MY FATHER'S KINGDOM

"Five stars to My Father's Kingdom. It's a rare read full of stunning turns of fate and unforeseen consequences that carry this satisfying saga through to its historically accurate conclusion — the long, bloody conflict between settlers and Indians that was "King Philip's War."

- Courtesy of Don Sloan, The Indie View

"Five stars…Reading historical fiction like My Father's Kingdom was a great experience…If you are interested in historical fiction, My Father's Kingdom: A Novel of Puritan New England by James W. George has everything and does not disappoint."

- Courtesy of Vernita Taylor, ReadersFavorite.com

"Five Stars…everything meshed together beautifully, staying accurate enough to the history of the war that happened while giving a unique and fresh tale to follow. It breathes life into the history we read so blandly, and George does an excellent way of making the scenario relatable and understandable to modern time."

- Courtesy of The Hungry Monster Review

"Tormented visions, Puritanical plots, and lost love all figure into the spirited narrative that brings the book's players alive — fully-fleshed human beings instead of mere footnotes in a dry, dusty history tome…This is a tale that will fully engage you on every level… This is high historical drama handled wonderfully by first-time author James W. George"

- Courtesy of PublishersDailyReviews.com

DEDICATED WITH LOVE AND GRATITUDE TO MY WIFE JENNIFER, MY CHILDREN KATRINA AND ZACHARY, AND TO PEACEMAKERS WHEREVER THEY MAY BE FOUND.

**JAMES W. GEORGE
JANUARY 2017**

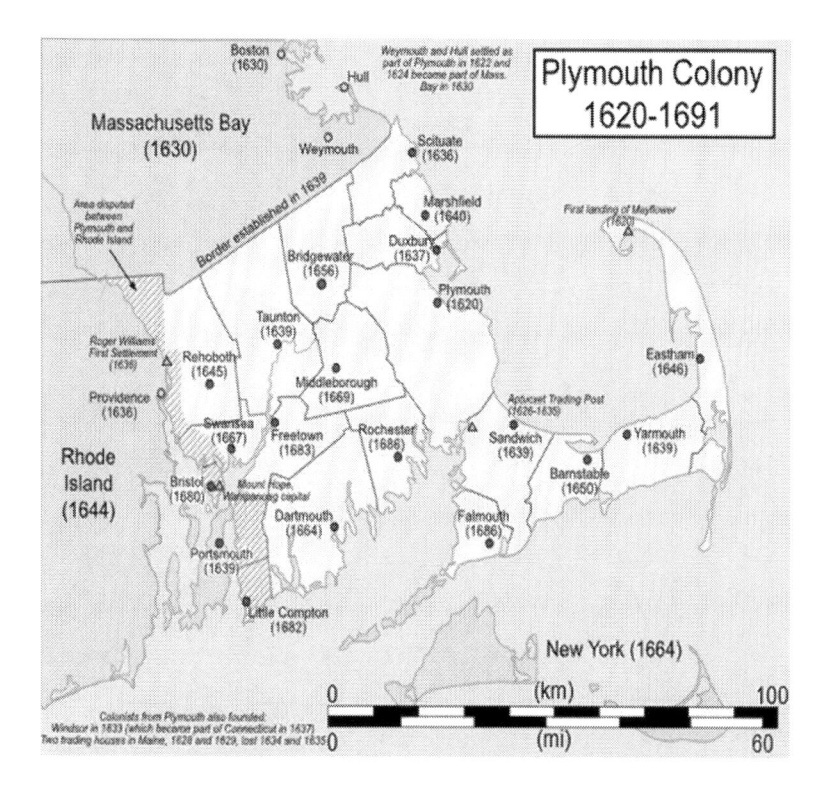

This map was created by Hoodinski. It is courtesy of Wikimedia Commons.

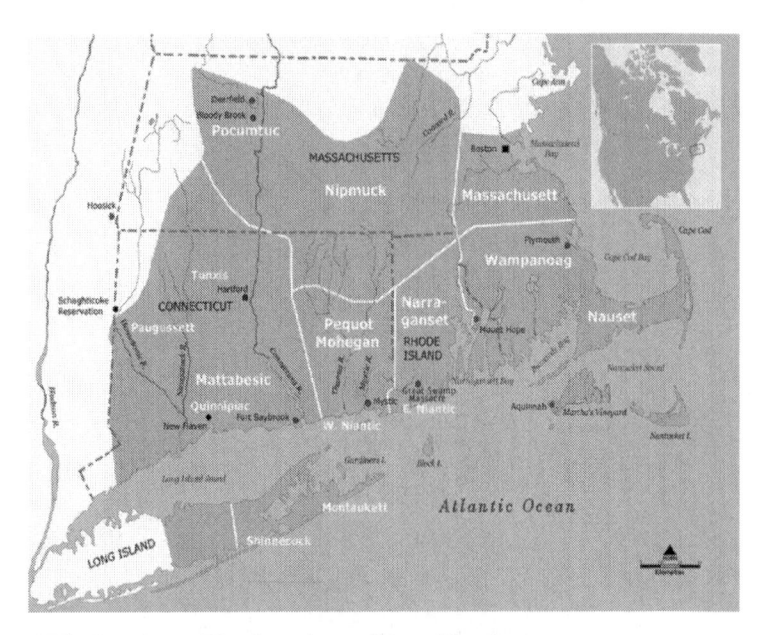

17th Century Native American Nations

Courtesy of Wikimedia Commons.

LIST OF CHARACTERS

(H) = Historical
(F) = Fictional

Barron, Jeremiah (F): A prominent member of the Plimoth General Court.

Brewster, Israel (F): A Puritan minister serving in the town of Middleborough in Plimoth Colony.

Brewster, William (H): Spiritual mentor of the original Pilgrims. Sailed to America on the Mayflower and died in 1644. Israel Brewster's grandfather.

Easton, John (H): The Deputy Governor of Rhode Island and prominent Quaker.

Eliot, John (H): A Puritan clergyman known for his missionary work among the Indians. He translated the Bible into their native language.

Farwell, Joshua and Mary (F): Joshua is a cooper in Middleborough. He and his wife seek the Reverend Brewster's counseling.

Fuller, Alice (F): A young woman residing in Middleborough.

Linto (F): A young powwas among the Wampanoag. Linto was adopted from the Abenaki people to the north. He is romantically involved with Wawetseka.

Massasoit (H): Also known as "Ossamequin." Massasoit

translates to "Great Sachem." Massasoit established the original alliance between the Wampanoag and the Pilgrims in the early 1620s. He was the father of Wamsutta and Metacomet and died in 1661.

Mather, Increase (H): A famous Puritan scholar and minister residing in Boston. He wrote a history of King Philip's War in 1676 and was involved in the Salem witch trials in 1692. He was the father of Cotton Mather.

Mattashunnamo (H): A friend of Tobias and his son Wampapaquan.

Mentayyup (F): One of the Wampanoag's most trusted and esteemed warriors. He was with Wamsutta in 1662 when the English summoned Wamsutta to Plimoth.

Metacomet (H): The Sachem of the Wampanoag. He is the son of Massasoit and the younger brother of Wamsutta. He assumed the role of Sachem after Wamsutta's death in 1662. At his father's request the English conferred the name of Philip upon him. He is the "King Philip" of King Philip's War.

Patuckson (H): A Christian Indian and friend of John Sassamon.

Phelps, Peter (F): A Puritan minister stationed in Plimoth.

Prence, Thomas (H): The governor of Plimoth Colony. He passed away in 1673.

Sachem (H): An honorary title similar to "Chief." Massasoit, Wamsutta, and Metacomet served as Sachems of the Wampanoag.

Sassamon, John (H): A Native American Christian who, due to his excellent English skills, frequently served as the liaison between the English and the Native Americans.

Tobias (H): One of Metacomet's most trusted Wampanoag advisors.

Wampapaquan (H): Tobias' young adult son.

Wamsutta (H): Son of Massasoit and older brother of Metacomet. He assumed the role of Sachem after Massasoit's death in 1661. Wamsutta perished under mysterious circumstances in 1662. At his father's request in 1660, the English conferred the name of Alexander upon him.

Wawetseka (F): A young spiritual leader among the Wampanoag. She is Linto's romantic partner.

Weetamoo (H): Wife of Wamsutta. She was also a prominent leader among the Wampanoag. Married to Petonowit after Wamsutta's death.

Wilder, Constance (F): A young adult Quaker residing in Providence.

Winslow, Josiah (H): The son of Mayflower passenger Edward Winslow. Josiah served as the leader of the colony's military forces, and became assistant governor in 1657. In 1673 he became governor.

Wootonekanuske (H): Wife of Metacomet and member of the council. She is Weetamoo's younger sister.

Part One
Spring 1671

"Welcome. Welcome Englishmen."
- Samoset, March 16, 1621

CHAPTER ONE

MONTAUP

"Hear my voice, Great Spirit, for I am as a son."

Silence. Linto strained his neck to cast his vision directly upward on a spectacular spring morning. The sky was remarkably clear and only the call of a white-throated sparrow dared to intrude upon his solitude. According to the English calendar, the month was May and the year was 1671. Linto prayed in Montaup and was a brisk walk away from Swansea in Plimoth Colony.

What an odd name for a place. Swansea. Although Linto's English was improving with each passing year, most things about their tongue continued to strike him as odd. Swannn-sea. Swansea. He was told there was another Swansea across the ocean. Once, at a missionary service, he asked if there was a sea of swans there, and the English ladies laughed until he blushed.

Linto knelt on the cool ground of the forest and communed with the Great Spirit. There was so much to be thankful for. He was strong, healthy, and a good provider for his people. The waters continued to teem with abundant fish and the crops had been planted. Although the winter was brutal, most among the Wampanoag had survived. And Linto, who had survived twenty-two winters, was in love.

Yet so much troubled Linto, and he constantly sought guidance from the Great Spirit. The Great Spirit itself caused him endless speculation and wonder. The Algonquin people called it "Kitchi Manitou" but also cautioned about "Wendigo," the demonic spirit. Could the English be corrupted by Wendigo? Could that explain their behavior? The Abenaki, who were once Linto's people, warned of Pamola, a fierce monster who lived on a mountain. And his adopted people, the Wampanoag, spoke of the giant Moshup who created the land, taught the people how to survive, and continued to influence their lives and destinies.

But why would the Great Spirit tolerate so much sadness and disease? Were the people being punished? Had his ancestors betrayed the Great Spirit by embracing the strange English from across the sea?

Why were the English possessed of such remarkable things, like enormous boats, knives of steel, and cooking pots that seemingly last forever? His people had an insatiable appetite for these wonders of the English, especially the alcohol. And the deadly, cruel guns.

Linto sighed and laid back on the soft ground, his eyes marveling at the tree tops. He had tasted the English alcohol three summers ago, and vomited all night. He could not comprehend the appeal and the desire, and he thanked the Great Spirit, for clearly it was the ruination of so many. There was so much about these people he would never understand. Their alcohol was vile and their language was strange. Their clothing often seemed absurd. Why did they treat their women as inferiors? In addition to it all, Linto strained to understand their God.

The English God seemed to permeate every aspect of their lives, but seemed to be a haze of contradictions. So many of Linto's people, the "Praying Indians" had embraced the English God and had been baptized as Christians, which seemed the quickest way to secure the good graces of the Englishmen. Linto had always been very attentive when the English clergymen discussed their God, (which seemed to be always) and when they pleaded with him to be baptized. Yet he was so far from understanding their God, whom they sometimes called Jehovah, and he was plagued with doubts.

If Jehovah got so angry that He flooded the entire world, wouldn't Linto's ancestors have known about it? Did a man really get swallowed by a whale and survive? Why did

Jehovah let his own Son be ridiculed and killed? Linto increasingly wondered if the language barrier was just too much, and he would never really understand these things.

"Are you dreaming again?" Linto should have been stunned and alarmed when his morning reverie was so suddenly shattered, but the voice was so beautiful it might have well been a message from the spirit world. He contemplated the question. Perhaps a morning this peaceful with a sky so blue was a dream after all. And now, the dream included Wawetseka.

Linto often tried to recall the day, or the month, or even the moment he realized he loved Wawetseka, but no distinct memory ever materialized. As far as he knew he had always loved her, from the time he was orphaned and adopted into the Wampanoag. She was the second daughter of Weetamoo, the wife and now widow of Wamsutta, the previous Sachem of his people. Her name translated into "pretty woman" and one might think it was the height of arrogance to name a child in such a manner, but Wamsutta the Sachem was prone to boasting, and nineteen summers later the name seemed absolutely prophetic.

"Linto, Linto, Linto," she laughed, and her mere presence instantly caused him to abandon and forget any serious thoughts on this morning. Linto often felt embarrassed and saddened by his name, as he would never know what his deceased parents really named him. Upon discovering him at a tender age in the midst of an Abenaki village, the Wampanoag were astonished to find a toddler smiling and singing, and henceforth he was Linto, the Abenaki word for "sing." Frequently he felt self-conscious about not having a manly Wampanoag name, but Wawetseka loved his name and called it out at every opportunity.

"Linto, Linto, Linto…staring at the sky again. Are you filled with troubles my love?" She sat next to him with her slender legs wrapped underneath her, and stared into his eyes.

"Not anymore." She forced a girlish giggle, and Linto privately groaned at his predictable lack of wit. They had been intimate with one another for months, but he still felt awkward and buffoonish in her presence.

"And what do the spirits tell you today, Linto?" Wawetseka knew how to convey a phrase with the perfect inflection, and presently she was conveying that she embraced the spirit world as devotedly as Linto. Her subtle tone, however, let him know there was no need for solemn isolation on such a day.

He understood precisely. "The spirits tell me it is probably time to rouse myself, and go hunting with Metacomet."

Metacomet. Proud, distinguished Metacomet was the Sachem of the Wampanoag. He was the younger brother of Wamsutta, and the son of the legendary Ossamequin. Ossamequin was known throughout the land as Massasoit, the "Great Sachem." It was Massasoit who allied the Wampanoag with the English, back when the English were new to the land, famished, and on the brink of extinction. Now it was the English who multiplied like fish in the sea.

Wawetseka took his hand. "I doubt the Sachem can have a hunting expedition without you." She giggled again. Despite the levity, they were both increasingly concerned about Metacomet.

Although eleven years younger than the thirty-three-year-old Sachem, Linto was renowned throughout the Wampanoag men as one of the most intelligent, and certainly the happiest. Despite his youth, Linto was quickly ascending as a trusted member of the Sachem's inner circle. His pending union with Wawetseka would establish him as a relative by marriage, as Metacomet was married to her aunt.

"And how is the Sachem's temperament today, Wawetseka?"

She remained silent, clearly crafting her words carefully. "I think he is in a dark place again, my love, but hopefully you can bring good cheer."

Metacomet had been the Sachem for nine summers, and Linto felt admiration and awe in his presence. He assumed the role of Sachem after the death of his brother, Wamsutta. Wamsutta's death was tragic and mysterious, and Metacomet, deep in his heart, would always blame the English for it. Whether that was reasonable or not Linto could not know. But he did know that when he looked upon Metacomet, he also felt a sense of sadness and pity, feelings that grew stronger with each passing day.

The Wampanoag were in trouble. Their lives, and the lives of their children, were ceaselessly worse. Although disease was not nearly as dire for them as it was for the parents of their parents, it was still a gruesome spectacle that haunted the people. Relationships with the Narragansett to the west, although currently peaceful, were fragile at best. And then there was the land.

In the time of Massasoit, when the starving English huddled in the cold, land seemed as plentiful as the sky. The Wampanoag hunted, fished, and farmed the land as their ancestors did. But the English came with so many marvelous things, and the trades seemed fruitful, wise, and so very easy. Land for knives and axes. Land for sturdy metal farm tools. Land for shoes, coats, and blankets. And soon the land was in short supply.

The pressures were weighing on the Sachem. Metacomet (or Philip, as the English called him) seemed to grow restless and angry as every new moon seemed to raise new questions about what the Wampanoag friendship with these English had truly wrought. Realizing his distracted silence, Linto resumed his attention on Wawetseka.

"Frankly I don't think I can raise his spirits these days. He seems so tormented and alone." He met Wawetseka's eyes.

"Well, Linto, you certainly raise my spirits," she whispered as she wrapped her arms around his shoulders. They fell to the ground in a lovers' embrace.

Lovestruck and clumsy, he finally managed his words. "I think the Sachem can find the deer without me this morning."

CHAPTER TWO

MIDDLEBOROUGH

"Lord God, hear Thou, thy humble prayers of thine people." Silence.

Reverend Israel Brewster scanned his congregation as they burst at the seams of the newly constructed meeting house, a mere half mile east of the Nemasket River. A gentle drizzle fell from the heavens as Reverend Brewster probed the families for any signs of restlessness or apathy. He had been in the pulpit for a mere ninety minutes and was not prepared to tolerate any lackluster attention.

He had been a pillar of the small but growing township of Middleborough in Plimoth Colony for four years now. The township was located fifteen miles west of Plimoth itself. It had seen so much change and growth in the previous decade that it changed its name three times. The original, native Nemasket became Middlebury, and most recently, Middlebury became Middleborough. During his first year in the pulpit Reverend Brewster genuinely believed if he asked three long-time residents the name of the township he would get four different answers.

He had prayed earnestly for divine guidance in the previous days regarding his sermon. Satan was working clearly and earnestly in their midst, and Reverend Brewster would ensure the deceiver gained no foothold in Middleborough. The twenty-eight-year-old clergyman had plenty of opportunities to observe sinfulness and wickedness in a typical week, and this one was no exception. Mending fences on the Sabbath. Public intoxication. Ostentatious attire. There was even some idle gossip about a poor depraved farmhand taking indecent liberties with livestock, which the reverend planned to ignore unless some concrete evidence somehow manifested itself via credible witnesses. Reverend Brewster was in no mood to revisit Leviticus 20:15 this week.

Instead, the preeminent theme from the pulpit this week would be love. Love and ministry, specifically ministering to the poor, deprived natives who still dwelled outside the loving light of the holy, true God. The men and women of this colony were a chosen people, miraculously delivered to this wilderness for God's own purpose, and Reverend Brewster would not hesitate to reinforce that fact.

The congregation was now singing Psalm 91, which always rendered blessed assurance, despite a sad, listless attempt at a baritone emanating from the pew of the Wentworth family. Perhaps they would benefit from additional tutelage in psalmody one evening this week. Enthusiasm was the key.

"You will not fear the terror of night
Nor the arrow that flies by day
Nor the pestilence that stalks in the darkness
Nor the plague that destroys at midday."

Reverend Brewster's attentions were quickly diverted from the unimpressive efforts of the Wentworths, and he was completely engaged by the lovely soprano of Alice Fuller, the comely, dark-eyed daughter of Roger Fuller. The Fullers had only left the mother country two years ago, and were renowned throughout Middleborough for their skill at smoking meats, and for their harpsichord, which was a delightful indulgence in a township like theirs. Alice had become so proficient at the instrument that the Fullers explored the notion of integrating it into Sunday worship. After careful consideration and consultation with the elders in Plimoth, Reverend Brewster conveyed the disappointing news that a harpsichord was deemed too popish and extravagant, and sincere, unornamented psalmody was the most Biblical and sincere mode of musical worship.

The psalmody wound down and the young clergyman

cleared his throat. The congregation gazed up with rapt attention as he prepared the next reading. Even after eighteen months, he detected an aura of pity and sadness in the eyes of the faithful when he spoke.

"Brothers and sisters, focus your attention with me." Reverend Brewster cut a marvelous figure in the pulpit, with his large blue eyes, straight and powerful back, and long black hair gently eclipsing his stiff white collar. "The holy book of Leviticus, chapter nineteen, verse thirty-three." He paused for dramatic effect as the cool rains began to escalate.

"And if a stranger sojourn with thee in your land, ye shall not vex him. But the stranger that dwelleth with you shall be unto you as one born among you, and thou shalt love him as thyself; for ye were strangers in the land of Egypt; I am the LORD your God.

"And brothers and sisters, is this sentiment not reinforced for us in the book of Exodus? For surely it is written in chapter twenty-three, verse nine:

"Also thou shalt not oppress a stranger; for ye know the heart of a stranger, seeing ye were strangers in the land of Egypt.

"And what strangers dwell among us in Plimoth colony? What shall we call them," he exclaimed, with dramatic emphasis on CALL. Reverend Brewster maintained careful eye contact and could not ignore the fact that thirty-four-year-old Isaac Reddington, the burly master carpenter, had lapsed into noisy slumber. He was hastened awake by his young daughter, whose eyes nervously darted across the spartan meeting house, fearing the timely wrath of the people. An attendant sauntered in his direction, armed with a goose feather fastened to a long birch rod, the standard implement for quelling slumber, via a subtle caress to the ear.

"Shall we call them strangers? Or natives? Perhaps we shall call them savages. Do you call them Wampanoag? Or Narragansett? Brothers and sisters, these words are of no consequence, for we certainly know who dwelleth amongst us. They are rightful children of God, and we are a chosen people, who, through the divine providence of the Almighty, have traversed thousands of miles and cruel winters and untold hardship, so that we may bring His glorious light.

"And what zeal have you brought to the task at hand? Does it exceed the zeal we've displayed in tending our livestock? Are we more inclined to dig wells for water, or to provide living water, so our kin shall not thirst? When the hand of the Wampanoag reaches out to you, are you prone to provide the word of God or a dram of rum for profit?" Reverend Brewster lingered excessively on "rum", doing his best to render it a two-syllable word, as if that helped make it all the more execrable. The first rum distillery opened in Boston a mere four years prior, and the clergy was convinced it might spell the death of the grand city on a hill.

"I renew my call for missionary zeal in this colony! Two Thursdays from today, I shall be travelling west to personally lead a missionary team, and Middleborough shall provide a dozen bold souls to teach English, prayer and psalmody. For now, congregation, let us conclude with a communal recitation of the Great Commission from the book of Matthew.

"And Jesus came and spake unto them, saying, All power is given unto me in heaven and in earth. Go ye therefore, and teach all nations, baptizing them in the name of the Father, and of the Son, and of the Holy Ghost."

The voices of the congregation echoed hypnotically from the rough-hewn rafters, and ended with a gentle "Amen."

CHAPTER THREE

MONTAUP

Metacomet had dreamt the dream again.

He stirred gently on that silent morning, before the restlessness began to overcome him. He surveyed the familiarity of his surroundings, hoping the comforts of home could help dislodge the anxiety brought about by the dream.

The Sachem's wetu was spacious but relatively modest. The saplings comprising the frame could be disassembled and relocated as circumstances dictated. The frame was perfectly circular, with a radius the length of four grown men. It was layered with superbly maintained sheets of bark, and the dwelling was warm and dry. It boasted a marvelous opening to the heavens that could easily accommodate the warmest of fires.

And Metacomet stared upward to the heavens. He slept without a fur, as spring was rapidly approaching summer. His ailing wife, Wootonekanuske, rose with a concerned stare.

"It is early, Husband. The strife and worries of the day can wait for the birds. And the light." Metacomet was silent and rose from his bench, nursing more pain and stiffness than was normal for one who had seen thirty-three summers. "The vision," he grunted, and resumed his silence.

Metacomet was a boy of seven summers and was running through the forest. He carried a spear that was too long for a boy twice his age, and he had adorned his face with the markings of his elders. He merrily tore through the undergrowth, the terror and bane of woodland creatures large and small. Exhausted, he took repose by a small stream and reached down to drink. Expecting to see the carefree visage of an ebullient child, the stream greeted him with the reflection of a wizened, gnarled old man bloodied by combat.

Towering over him, standing taller than no Wampanoag had ever stood, was Wamsutta.

His brother beamed with a smile that could light the night, and with nary an effort, playfully nudged Metacomet with his powerful hands until Metacomet was face down in the cool water. Laughing hysterically, Wamsutta chanted, "sleepy boy, tiny boy, time for your nap," the same taunt he tormented his younger brother with as a youth.

Metacomet growled and gave chase as the sky faded to a burnt purple unlike any he had seen. He ran as fast as his tiny legs would propel him, without a chance of catching his brother, who continued shouting as loud as thunder, "sleepy boy, tiny boy, time for your nap."

Soon Wamsutta approached a towering cliff but made no effort to slow or alter his path. If anything, he was infused with a burst of new, maddening energy and began accelerating. He leapt off the cliff, and spreading his arms as a mighty bird, he soared upwards until he was almost out of sight. Metacomet would not let this challenge go uncontested, and he repeatedly shouted the name the English bestowed upon his brother in the year preceding his death: "Alexander! Alexander! Alexander!" Metacomet soared off the cliff and plummeted like a falling stone until falling into his unconscious body back in his wetu.

Wootonekanuske remained silent and tried to ascertain the proper approach. Although sympathetic to her Sachem's torments, she dreaded the visions, as they were usually followed by prolonged irritability and isolation.

"But much was different this time," she inquired in a calming and empathetic tone. Metacomet rubbed his temples.

"But somehow the same," he replied. How many times had the vision visited him in the nine summers since Wamsutta left him? Four? Five? Sometimes the dream was set in a torrential rain. Sometimes Metacomet was older. But they all ended the same, with Wamsutta soaring to the heavens and leaving his younger brother dashed and alone. Clearly the meaning was profound, and the dream was a voice from the spirit world. Metacomet needed insight and wisdom.

"Assemble the council."

Wootonekanuske sighed. As the younger sister of Wamsutta's widow Weetamoo, the fate of the former Sachem almost caused her as much grief as Metacomet. But this insistent wallowing in an unknowable tragedy was not healthy for her husband, and it was not healthy for the Wampanoag. She knew, however, the futility of trying to dissuade her husband at moments like this.

"And make certain Linto is there," he commanded as he left the wetu.

After a morning meal of trout and squash, the council of the Wampanoag gathered at the large formation of quartz rock at Mountaup as they had done so often. The formation conveyed an almost unnatural beauty, culminating in a semi-circular chasm at its base that evoked an ancient throne. The site was ideal as the summit of the hill was higher than twenty men, and it gave the people an unobstructed view of Narragansett Bay and the approach of any hostile intruders. The English, with their penchant for renaming everything they touch and see, referred to it as Mount Hope.

There were seven participants in the council that day. Wootonekanuske held a place of esteem, as did the venerable Mentayyup, whose reputation as the strongest, fiercest warrior was still unchallenged, though he was six summers older than the Sachem. Tobias, one of Metacomet's closest confidants, was present with his incessant scowl. Waatla, the eldest, sat on the ground. She had anglicized her name in recent years and was now called Willa. No one knew precisely how old Willa was, but it was a remarkable number since she so clearly remembered the arrival of the first English ship at Patuxet, back when they seemed so strange and pitiful.

Linto was there, despite the overt glares of resentment from council elders, who silently contemplated the injustice that such a young man who had accomplished so little was evolving into one of the Sachem's most trusted colleagues. Wussausmon, as expected, was present as well.

Wussausmon, known by the English name "John Sassamon," had demonstrated a remarkable inclination for learning the English language and religion. He was known by the colonists as a "Praying Indian," the term they used for Christian converts. It was a term some would say denoted respect, whereas others used it with an element of derision.

Sassamon grew up as an indentured servant to an English family, and his insights into their language, customs, and religion had proven invaluable. It was little wonder he served as the Sachem's closest advisor regarding written deeds, wills, trade agreements, and real estate transactions. He had even attended the English sanctum of learning, which they called Harvard.

"I want to hear the story again Mentayyup." Metacomet was so restless he could scarcely frame his thoughts. Fortunately, Mentayyup had experienced this discussion numerous times and knew exactly what was being asked of him.

"Sachem, please. The events were so long ago and I have nothing new to add. Nothing has changed." Metacomet cast one of his infamous glares his way, a storehouse of rage and contempt so intimidating the powerful Mentayyup almost quivered. He quickly relented.

"Sachem, it was nine summers ago, as you know. Your brother had been Sachem for scarcely one summer since your father departed our world. And you had grown to be an esteemed member of the people, showing tremendous wisdom for your twenty-four summers. So you remember how difficult things were. We felt so lost without the great Massasoit. Some felt he could never leave us." Metacomet stared at the ground as the council stood silently, recalling the seemingly endless tears and grief of his passing.

Mentayyup continued. "I remember the hardships. We believed there would always be endless fur to keep the English happy, and we would always trade for their cookware, their knives, blankets, and clothes. No one imagined the fur could be depleted so quickly."

"I remember it clearly," commented the Sachem. "Our traps grew emptier every new moon." Metacomet tried to maintain a neutral, inquisitive bearing. He remembered the events of Wamsutta's final days very well, but over the years he constantly interrogated his advisors for any new insight or clue that may guide him on the shadowy path ahead.

"You were there, Mentayyup. At the hunting camp on the shore of Munponset pond."

Mentayyup looked even more somber and distraught. "Yes, Sachem. There were eight of us with Wamsutta at the camp. It had been a glorious week, and the game was plentiful. You and Tobias were at the camp at Titicut."

Metacomet hung on every word. There was almost no one he trusted more than Mentayyup. Like Metacomet, as a child Mentayyup had been adopted into the wolf clan of the Wampanoag. His people raised their children as members of five distinctive clans: The wolf, the bear, the deer, the snipe and the turtle. The lifelong distinction was awarded based on the predilections and aptitudes of the children. Members of the wolf clan were renowned as leaders and warriors.

Children of the bear clan were healers and practitioners of medicine. As children, they were often observed picking and identifying plants and berries. The deer clan were providers. The boys of the deer clan probably grew up pretending to hunt, whereas the girls showed aptitude in gardening and cooking. The snipe clan were the builders. Snipe children were easy to identify as they were always digging, gathering sticks and piling rocks. A spiritual leader of the tribe, or a "powwas," emanated from the turtle clan. These children were quickly identified for their quiet, contemplative but inquisitive mannerisms. Metacomet felt he desperately needed the wisdom of the turtle clan today.

Mentayyup continued recounting the events from that fateful week. "Despite the troubles of the day, your brother was inspired. He was in a glorious mood, and he instilled a sense of confidence and harmony among us."

Metacomet bristled at the traces of sycophancy from such an esteemed warrior, but his intentions were pure. Wamsutta had established his leadership firmly and righteously, ensuring stability for a people still reeling from the loss of his father.

The tale continued. "It was after mid-day when we were skinning and drying the morning's game when Winslow appeared from nowhere."

Winslow. No matter how many times Metacomet recounted the last days of his brother, he always grimaced at the mere sound. Winslow. Like so many of these sanctimonious English, Josiah Winslow had learned nothing from his father, the esteemed Governor Edward Winslow. Father Edward was a man of peace and patience and a friend to Massasoit and the Wampanoag. He earned the trust of English and Wampanoag alike and was elevated to the position of governor.

Josiah the son, though elevated to the role of deputy governor of Plimoth, was boastful and arrogant and no friend to Metacomet's people. Like so many of his countrymen, Josiah Winslow was quick to forget the eternal debt the English owed Massasoit, and he arrogantly viewed all the tribal nations as one entity, hostile to the English, and hostile to their incessant hunger for land.

Mentayyup was anxious to continue. "It was remarkable how Winslow emerged from the woods without warning. All these years I've wondered if he was genuinely in search of Wamsutta, or if he randomly stumbled upon us while on another errand. He was accompanied by two young militiamen who resembled frightened rabbits. How their hands shook as they gripped their muskets. Naturally, the eight of us surrounded the Sachem and reached for our firearms. Your brother would have none of it however. He exclaimed that friend Winslow should be welcomed, and the friendship of their fathers must never be forsaken." Metacomet visibly bristled at the phrase "friendship of their fathers."

Linto's eyes seemed to widen as Mentayyup continued. "Things were very tense because all were aware of son Winslow's growing animosity to Wamsutta. That was when Wamsutta had tired of the Plimoth monopoly on the sale of our lands and had sold some small tracts to the Quakers of the west. For some reason Plimoth found this infuriating."

Linto blinked, trying to grasp what was being said. He knew he had no business interrupting, but his curiosity overwhelmed him. "Quakers?" he muttered inquisitively.

Sassamon, sensing the lull, never missed an opportunity to show off his remarkable knowledge of the English. "You are young, Linto, and may not know of the Quakers. They are the English west of here among the Narragansett. They are different in their ways than the men of Plimoth and Boston."

Linto, as usual, felt baffled but intrigued by the strange ways of these foreigners. He felt his question so stupid it was barely audible. "So they quake a lot? Are they cold? Isn't that what it means to quake?"

Sassamon refrained from any condescension. "They worship the English God differently, and the men of Plimoth got mad and sent them west. They actually call themselves the Society of Friends."

Tobias guffawed and spoke for the first time. "They fear the Quakers in Plimoth even more than us. But not as much as the French Catholics. Oh, how the Plimoth English despise the Catholics. Sometimes for fun I like to tell a farmer we've had Catholics in our village for a feast. Just to watch their heads spin. But you can trust a Quaker man. Not like all those other Christians." Tobias was gently rocking, and Linto suspected he had been drinking rum.

Linto was almost sorry he asked the question. Quakers. Baptists. Catholics. Willa had even told him once the men of Plimoth and Boston are constantly angry with one another about church things. Evidently one of them was not "separate" enough from the bad ways of England. How could this God be causing so much confusion?

There was an awkward silence which the council seemed in no hurry to end. Each individual was deep in thought and anxious about where Metacomet was leading them. Finally, without prodding, Mentayyup resumed. "Wamsutta quickly defused any tensions, and we left our guns untouched. But no matter how cordial and accommodating our Sachem was, Winslow was angry and full of accusations. It was difficult for us to follow, since none of us spoke the English language as well as Wamsutta. Still, it was pretty clear what was transpiring. Some of the words I understood were *Alexander, forbidden…trust…land…and Plimoth.*

"Winslow was driving his finger into Wamsutta's chest and raising his voice. I was quick to anger at that time and impulsively jumped in front of Winslow, my face a mere hand's length from his. *RESPECT* was the English word I yelled, as loudly as my lungs would permit. Winslow was shocked and fell backwards like a frightened mouse. His underlings leered at one another, mouths agape, each unsure what should be done.

"I did not mean for Winslow to be so humiliated, but his ways were unacceptable. Our eight men were rushing forth for conflict once again when Wamsutta violently pushed me away. *SHAME, Mentayyup* he called out, and he pulled Winslow up from the ground. *SHAME* he shouted again and glared at me with indignation."

"*Winslow is the son of Winslow the father. He is a friend and ally to all our people. He is our guest and we were in deliberations. His people are concerned about some minor sales of lands that they wish to be consulted on.*"

Mentayyup continued. "Winslow and Wamsutta spoke continuously, with Winslow's voice rising once again and Wamsutta smiling and shaking his head. Finally, Wamsutta addressed us.

"*Friend Winslow the son has grave concerns about rumors and falsehoods. The people of Plimoth have heard wild allegations of double-dealing among our people. Allegations of ill-fated alliances to do harm to Winslow's people. Allegations of fraudulent land sales. And now friend Winslow is questioning the loyalties of me, Wamsutta, son of the greatest friend the Plimoth English have ever known.*

"*I will be accompanying friend Winslow back to Plimoth. He has invited me to camp and dine with him at his home as an honored guest. I will travel to the court at Plimoth to reassure our friends the Englishmen of the trust and loyalty of our nation.*"

Mentayyup continued. "Instantly I volunteered to accompany the Sachem. I suggested an escort of four of us, with the remaining four returning home. He only shook his head solemnly.

"*No Mentayyup, I am thankful, but it is not appropriate. For me to travel with armed escorts sends a bad signal to our Plimoth friends. I must take this journey alone. It is urgent I send the strongest message that the Wampanoag are the most reliable friends of Plimoth, and I fully trust the hospitality of Winslow. We will converse as our fathers have done before us.*"

Metacomet cursed under his breath. "And you permitted this madness Mentayyup? Couldn't you see Winslow was forcing him?"

Mentayyup was renowned for maintaining a state of quiet dignity, and he was proud of the deference and respect he showed to the leader of his people. At this instance, however, years of regret and sorrow burst to the surface in a rage-filled outburst. "Metacomet, you have heard me tell the tale ten times! You know every detail and so does Tobias and Willa and Wootonekanuske and Sassamon! How many times have I testified how I begged Wamsutta to let me accompany him? How I pleaded and cried out until he reprimanded me for my insubordination! You know all of this and yet here we are again and again!"

The council held their breath, anticipating the wrath of Metacomet would be instantaneous and awesome. Instead, once again, the silence was agonizing yet welcome. Linto was sure he saw a tear stream down his Sachem's cheek.

Finally, Metacomet spoke, and they all labored to hear. "Time and time again we revisit the tragedy. Just when I am certain of my hatred, the doubts rise. The visions come. How I wish there was just a detail, an unturned stone that would chart my course." He briefly cast his gaze skyward and then stared at the ground. "I am sorry Mentayyup. I have never questioned your bravery and your strength. Continue. We must all hear your words. And some were too young at the time to fully understand these events." Metacomet cast a glance at Linto, much to the visible disgust of Tobias.

Mentayyup bowed his head and resumed the tale in a somber and reserved tone. "Wamsutta instructed us to anticipate his return to Montaup in ten days. He would be accompanied by Winslow and a trading party, and we would feast together. And without another word they were gone. I know your next question and my answer has never wavered. He looked powerful. He was not fatigued, or feverish, or stressed with sickness. Wamsutta when he left us was…magnificent."

Mentayyup continued his account of that tragic week. After Wamsutta left with Winslow and the "young frightened rabbits," Mentayyup assumed an uneasy role of awkward leadership. He led the dispirited band as they gathered the spoils of the hunting and broke camp for Montaup. Mentayyup did his best to elevate their spirits, attempting to exude the confident knowledge that Wamsutta was always right in these matters and their alliance with Plimoth was strong.

Upon returning home and conveying the account to Wamsutta's wife, the renowned Weetamoo, it soon became evident that she advocated an entirely different course of action and was not concerned about any reprimands for insubordination from her husband. Within the blink of an eye she had likened Winslow to three different animals and associated animal parts (Mentayyup clearly recalled something about the genitals of a skunk), and she had directed the assembly of eighty Wampanoag warriors who would accompany her to Plimoth the next morning.

At the time Mentayyup knew he would feel shame if Weetamoo banned him from the expedition for his foolhardiness, and shame if he went and bore the enraged glare of Wamsutta when they arrived with eighty men and the English scurried for their muskets. For better or worse Weetamoo rendered no directive on the matter, and naturally Mentayyup went.

The journey to Plimoth took two days. Needless to say, Plimoth sentries were alarmed, bells were furiously rung, militiamen gathered, but blessedly no altercation transpired as Weetamoo firmly and decisively conveyed they were there for Wamsutta, and nothing else.

After tense negotiations with a captain of the militia, it was determined Weetamoo could enter the inner sanctum of Plimoth accompanied by eight men. She was greeted by Skunk Genitals Winslow, looking downcast and skulking. Winslow recounted the tale of his own hospitality at his home in Mattakessett, the place of many fish, which the English called Duxbury. But allegedly Wamsutta became so fatigued by the journey to Mattakesett he was unable to sup with

Winslow and his family and took no nourishment.

The next morning, he was still not desirous of food or beverage but felt adequate to make the journey to Plimoth. Winslow claimed he begged Wamsutta to rest for another day, but Wamsutta was adamant that his stamina was fine and Winslow should not question it. A physician was summoned, Doctor Fuller, who had received extensive medical training in the mother country. Doctor Fuller offered Wamsutta a distinctive-smelling liquid in a clay jar which he called a "portion of working physic" and said Wamsutta should consume it if the humours of his body were not in balance by nightfall.

A horse was arranged, and Wamsutta made the journey to Plimoth, where, after briefly appearing before the Plimoth General Court, he was still unwilling and unable to accept nourishment. He fell into a deep slumber with episodes of fever and delirium that evening and had not emerged from bed since.

Skunk Genitals Winslow led the group to a comfortable cabin where they found their Sachem barely maintaining consciousness, "guarded" by a timid-looking young man with enormous blue eyes. Weetamoo always found the variation of eye color among these foreigners to be fascinating, and her gaze lingered on the hapless youngster who appeared agonized and distraught. His blue eyes travelled from her to the bed and she followed them hypnotically.

Wamsutta was indeed in desperate straits, and Winslow, whose knowledge of the native language was always poor, received an education in profane Wampanoag rage that, had he been able to understand, rendered him several levels below skunk genitals in the divine order of the universe. He muttered relentlessly about how the physicians had been attending him, how they had done everything possible, and they were confident Wamsutta was improving.

Weetamoo would hear none of it, however, and she

effortlessly took command of the situation. Soon their beloved Sachem was being transported back to Montaup via a quickly devised litter. Skunk Genitals was yammering about offering horses, escorts and physicians, but she paid him no heed.

Wamsutta would never again utter a word to his beloved Weetamoo, nor to his trusted Mentayyup, nor to any of his people. Shortly before sunset, near the north side of the Snipatuet Pond, the great son of Massasoit, anointed as "Alexander" by their English allies, Sachem of his people, took his last earthly breath and was committed to the spirit world of their ancestors.

Mentayyup's account was finally complete and he seemed emotionally drained. Metacomet had been standing solemnly still and focusing obsessively on every word. He now began to pace frantically as he was apt to do. He rubbed his powerful hands through his thick mane of jet black hair. "Winslow…the physician. A *portion of working physic*. Such trickery. How they ooze falsehood like tree sap. Never. Never. He was never sick, not for a day. Not by the English diseases, not by anything. Poison."

Tobias had stopped his rocking and his cold eyes raged. "That was the time, Sachem. That was the time to punish the English. We all knew."

The weeks and months following Wamsutta's death had been a turbulent time. Power struggles ensued as Metacomet rose to authority and consolidated loyalty. Weetamoo, widowed and enraged, demanded swift and unquestioned vengeance against a nation of cowardly murderers. But young Metacomet deferred. He was cautious. He was grief-stricken, losing his father and older brother in such a short-time. And Wamsutta's demise would always linger, causing feelings of doubt, grief, confusion and helplessness throughout the people.

But most of all Metacomet heard the words of the great

Massasoit: "The Plimoth English are our most cherished allies. No one else can provide us with such marvelous things. And when I, Massasoit, was a young man, and our people were ravaged and depleted by disease, who stood with us against the wrath of the Narragansett? Bradford. Brewster. Winslow. Plimoth." Metacomet's reverie was interrupted as Tobias was growing more boisterous.

"That was the time, Sachem! Of course he was poisoned. But the time should be now! Or it will be never! The English just buy and buy, and take and take. There is a new boatload every week! They are like mosquitos. Plimoth has betrayed us, and it is time to send the English back across the sea."

Sassamon shook his head in disbelief. "Lunacy! Blasphemy! Be silent, you drunkard! Look what the English have brought us. A whole new world of understanding, and the light of Christ. Look at their shipbuilding, their firearms, and their iron tools. And you wish to reject that? You wish to fight them? It would be a disaster. And why should we fight? Because Wamsutta got sick and perished nine summers ago?"

Tobias kept his rage in check. "Because he was poisoned nine summers ago, and everything gets worse every summer. The English are laughing at us. They will never have enough land. They will hate us and revile us until we dress like fools from head to toe as they do, learn to read their big, ancient book, and eat their bread and wine."

"And we would be slaughtered if we embrace this madness. What became of the Pequot? How many were sold off in chains?" Sassamon paused to let the memory of the Pequot resonate. "Stop this crazy talk of poison and murder and warfare. And let me teach you the big, ancient book. It is clear to all that you are desperately in need of wisdom."

At that moment, all seemed certain that Tobias would shred the learned Christian apart right there in front of the council. Fortunately for Sassamon, the Sachem majestically

held his hand high in the air, and promptly ended the conflict.
	"Enough. I have heard enough today. Linto!" All cast their eyes upon Linto, whom they thought might dash away in a panic.
	"Linto, walk with me."

CHAPTER FOUR

MIDDLEBOROUGH

Daylight?

It seemed an impossibility, but Israel Brewster, to his chagrin, had slept well past sunrise and would now be rushed during his morning ritual. He was clearly weary after his labors in the pulpit yesterday, and the communal meals and Sabbath activities often did not seem nearly as restful as they were intended to be.

He rose and knew at once he had been dreaming of her, yet could not recollect a solitary detail. At one time such dreams provided a sense of solace and joy, but as of late they only seemed to inflict numb resignation. He washed his pale face in his basin and silently went to prayer, thanking the Lord for his health, for the community, and for another day.

His scripture reading was unusually brief due to the late hour. He read four chapters of the book of Joshua and contemplated how best to integrate them into his future sermons. He also considered the upcoming missionary service and gave careful thought to planning that day's activities.

Reverend Brewster nourished himself quickly and rapidly with a sampling of smoked meats presented on Saturday by the Fuller family, along with a quarter loaf of oat bread dripping with butter. Time was of the essence, but he would need his strength as he was committed to a home raising all morning and spiritual counseling in the afternoon. The day would be taxing indeed, he thought, and devoured another quarter loaf.

He dressed quickly but before leaving his modest home he permitted himself the brief luxury of one of Sarah's letters, from two years ago. He skimmed it casually until arriving at the conclusion, a sonnet that he whispered aloud as his heart raced.

> *For blessed are we, creatures made anew*
> *Lovers made one in a strange, divine land*
> *Through strife and turmoil we are hand in hand*
> *We are joyous; our love forever true.*

His hand was trembling slightly as he gently filed away the letter, and Israel Brewster began his day with the community of Middleborough.

After a vigorous four-minute walk, he arrived later than he had hoped, but not egregiously so. Other families were arriving with anxious children and baskets of food. Today they would raise a house for the Barnstrom family, as Hope Barnstrom was clearly blessed with a third child which should be born before the winter arrived.

After everyone was gathered, Reverend Brewster spoke a brief prayer, giving thanks to the Almighty for the health and talents of the community, and for a day free of rain. He sought the Lord's blessing for the Barnstrom family and their new home, and for the joyfully anticipated birth of their third child.

Now the day's work would commence. What seemed to be a small army had prepositioned tools, timber and brick. Reverend Brewster would like to seize this opportunity to demonstrate to the congregation that he was much more than a slender, classically educated bookworm and could easily wield an axe, raise rafters and cut mortises and tenons as well as the next man, but the fact was he was about as useful as a thunderstorm in these situations, with his clumsy and inefficient hands, and his increasingly failing vision. No lack of skill, however, would deter the good reverend as his threw himself into the labors at hand with hearty enthusiasm and blessed humility.

The stone footing had been set last week, and the sills

were being set upon them. The home would be classic Plimoth construction, with timber framing, mortise and tenon fastening, "wattle and daub" construction for the walls, and clapboards encasing the entire home.

Today would hopefully mark the completion of the framing, with the intent to transition to dinner and evening prayer by sunset. Most of the detailed mortise and tenon work would be accomplished by the ruddy and burly carpenter Reddington, who was so somnolent and disinterested in worship, yet so pleasing in God's eye while woodworking.

The ends of the enormous corner posts were charred in the time-tested tradition of the colonies. As the morning faded to afternoon, the heat of the day (atypical for spring, but delightful nonetheless), crept slowly and inevitably, but nothing would deter the progress of the community. Reverend Brewster circulated throughout the work site, providing encouragement, carrying timber, and shouting exhortations. Men worked furiously with their adzes, the perpendicular axe that their ancestors had used to smooth timber since before the time of Christ.

Brewster knew his schedule would not quite permit an entire day dedicated to the home. In the late afternoon before dinner he would be counseling members of the congregation, and he hoped the physical labors of the day would be channeled into mental acuity and insight in order to best serve his parishioners. He hoped he could at least be present to assist in the raising of the frame, which would hopefully commence well before his departure.

He had begun sweating profusely, certainly more profusely than was warranted relative to the magnitude of his physical work. He wiped his brow and was delighted when the comely visage of Alice Fuller approached with a pewter mug of cool water. Smiling, she extended her delicate hand.

"You certainly appear parched, Reverend." Her deep

brown eyes glowed with the joys of youth and health.

"Alice, you are most thoughtful, and the mug is appreciated." Brewster made no pretense of civility, and devoured the refreshing water in one mighty gulp. Handing the pewter back to her, he hoped to convey his gratitude once again in a witty, inviting fashion that would compel the twenty-year old Alice to remain and converse, but his mind was a blank slate. He locked eyes with her and gazed upon her wondrous, delicate features. Perhaps the heat had rendered his senses deficient, but it was clear that not only was he tongue-tied, but he had lost all perspective of time and had no inkling how long he stared, until at last the awkward silence was broken by the giggling of Alice's young sister Elizabeth. Brewster's cheeks were flush with embarrassment and he muttered about returning to work.

By three in the afternoon, well after a rushed lunch of fowl, venison and squash, it was apparent the work had progressed remarkably well. The two frames, the front and the back, or the "bents" as the carpenters referred to them, had been completed and the ropes had been fastened. This was the part of the day Brewster found exhilarating. Fewer things provided a sense of camaraderie and accomplishment than when dozens of men united around the bents, and raised them high off the ground.

Some would be pulling with the ropes and others pushing with poles. Brewster delighted in manning a rope, and the sight of the bents being raised as the workers propelled them upward filled his heart with joy, for seemingly at that moment, a new home was born.

Realistically, however, a great deal of work was still to be done. Powerful, unwieldy horizontal beams known as girts would be raised to fasten the front and rear bents together. Rafters would be added and connected by the collar beams. It was a stunning amount of work to be completed in a day, and there would be several weeks of earnest labor to turn the frame into a home.

Brewster paid his regards to the townsfolk, prepared his departure, and extended his congratulations for their outstanding work. He prayed once more with the Barnstrom family, and beseeched the Almighty that this new home would be employed in His service.

He arrived back at his home by four in the afternoon. He vigorously washed his face and hands in his basin and refreshed himself with a modest serving of small beer. He prayed in silence for guidance and wisdom, so he may provide worthy counsel to the community.

Reverend Brewster provided formal counseling once a week to all who had cause to seek him out. Often advice was sought for matters quite trivial, but at times members of the flock were genuinely anguished. It was vital that worldly matters be resolved as expeditiously and quietly as possible, because civil matters such as property, child-rearing, and matrimonial strife were quickly elevated to the municipal government, and ungodly behavior would certainly be rectified in a public fashion.

Brewster sat in silence for a good ten minutes. He enjoyed the intimacy of his home when providing counsel of clergy, as it frequently lent itself to a sense of candor and equanimity not found in the meeting house. He began to wonder if any would seek his counsel on a busy day as today, but soon Josiah Franklin made his appearance.

Josiah was a gaunt man of approximately fifty years with a long face, a crooked nose and piercing gray eyes. He was never shy about soliciting counsel, especially when there was suspicious activity afoot. His livelihood was his modest farm, and he was proud of his corn crops and livestock. After brief obligatory pleasantries, he arrived at the heart of the matter.

"What can be done to block out the witchcraft of the savages, Reverend?"

Reverend Brewster sighed, possibly more loudly than he intended. He knew the wickedness of Satan's power, and knew witchcraft was a serious matter indeed. Exodus 22:18 (*Thou shalt not suffer a witch to live*) was emblazoned upon his heart at a very young age, and he constantly encouraged the congregation to be vigilant and intolerant of sorcery and evil spells. But often he wondered if, perhaps, there was a little too much witchcraft transpiring in their tiny hamlet.

"Tell me more, Josiah."

"Well, you know how difficult the times are. My third boy's fever had finally broken last week, so the entire family was able to help plant the corn, thank heaven. We were laboring in the south field, by the Nemasket road, and sure enough, there were at least a half dozen savages strolling by, on their way to only God knows where."

"Wampanoag? Nipmuc? Narragansett?"

"Savages, Reverend. That's all I know. And I'm sorry to say I caught the eye of an old one, an old lady. And she just stared. Oh, how she stared, Reverend. Her stare could chill a man to the bone. What a wicked, withered old thing she was."

"She stared at you?"

"No, at my biggest cow. She was all alone there in the south field, and this squaw just would not take eyes off her. She stared and stared. I thought she was going to devour her with her eyes. Oh, my poor Annabel."

A deep sigh. "Josiah...."

"And now? A week later? Dead. Oh, how she suffered with the bovine pneumonia, Reverend. There was nothing I could do. The hatred I feel for that witch. How do I block her spells? Can we string her up?"

"Josiah, witchcraft is a very serious matter, and I'm afraid an icy stare and a dead cow do not rise to the requisite level of evidence in this colony to prosecute witchcraft. Perhaps we should instead give thanks for your son's renewed health, and perhaps supplications are in order for the continued prosperity of your farm."

Josiah's long crooked nose seemed even more misshapen as he lashed out. "I don't want supplications Reverend, I want justice! And I mean to take this up with the government in Plimoth."

"I cannot stop you Josiah, but I am confident that path will not pay dividends. Will you read scripture with me?" Josiah hung his head mournfully. He felt ashamed for raising his voice to a man of God, a man so committed to hearing his troubles. The pressure and strain of the farm had seemed overwhelming. His entire family spent what seemed to be the entire winter in the thralls of some form of disease and fever. Last year's corn harvest was meager at best. And now a cherished cow had perished with pneumonia, perhaps the first of many. He nodded his head meekly.

"Josiah, I turn to the Proverbs in troubled times. Let's reflect and pray on the third chapter."

"*My son, forget not my law; but let thine heart keep my commandments. For length of days, and long life, and peace, shall they add to thee. Let not mercy and truth forsake thee: bind them about thy neck; write them upon the table of thine heart. So shalt thou find favour and good understanding in the sight of God and man.*

"*Trust in the Lord with all thine heart; and lean not unto thine own understanding. In all thy ways acknowledge him, and he shall direct thy paths. Be not wise in thine own eyes: fear the Lord, and depart from evil. It shall be health to thy navel, and marrow to thy bones. Honour the Lord with thy substance, and with the first fruits of all thine increase. So shall thy **barns be filled with plenty**, and thy presses shall burst out with new wine.*"

"Farmer Franklin, I am praying for you. I am praying for your farm, for your family, and yes, even for your cattle."

"Reverend Brewster…I….Israel." Josiah felt excessively informal addressing his pastor by his first name. "Thank you. But please be reminded I do not take witchcraft among the savages lightly."

"Nor do I, Josiah. Good evening to you."

Reverend Brewster accompanied his guest through the front door, and bid him farewell once again. He lingered in front of his modest home and basked in the cool of the evening. He was expecting one more counseling session this evening, and Mr. and Mrs. Farwell soon strode up his path.

Joshua Farwell was a twenty-five-year-old cooper. Like many in the township, his livelihood was certainly not tied exclusively to one pursuit, and he maintained a viable living with basic carpentry, hunting, and occasional sea service. His bride Mary was a delightful lass, and Brewster would always mentally picture her as a young bride, since he performed their ceremony a mere eight months ago. This was their first time seeking counsel, and neither seemed happy at the prospect.

"I hope we're not a bother, Reverend," chimed Mary, her eyes fixed upon his front door. "I know you must be worn from all your labors today."

"Nonsense, Mary, nonsense. As the Proverbs remind us, *the soul of the sluggard desireth, and hath nothing: but the soul of the diligent shall be made fat*." Mary giggled at the notion of "fat" in the Old Testament, and Reverend Brewster almost blushed. "Of course, *be made prosperous* may be a more accurate translation, but then again…" Brewster gently tapped his abdomen to imply hearty appetite but the gesture didn't quite resonate due to his lanky frame.

"Joshua, Mary, do come in. You both look marvelous, the Lord has truly kept you. Come and sit in the front room." Joshua's eyes darted nervously and he remained silent as he followed his petite wife into the home. After a brief prayer, the reverend gently probed the nature of their visit, but he had learned over the years only the most delicate of inquiry was usually required to evoke candor from his guests.

"And how be thy marital bliss, Joshua? If you recall

my guidance, a young man should read Proverbs 31 at least once a week during his first year of matrimony. My goodness, this has become an evening of Proverbs. Let's read it together, shall we? Starting with verse ten, of course:

"Who can find a virtuous woman? For her price is far above rubies. The heart of her husband doth safely trust in her, so that he shall have no need of spoil. She will do him good and not evil all the days of her life. She seeketh wool, and flax, and worketh willingly with her hands. She is like the merchants' ships; she bringeth her food from afar. She riseth also while it is yet night, and giveth meat to her household, and a portion to her maidens...."

"Reverend," Mary muttered gently under her breath, anxious to get to the heart of the matter but equally averse to interrupting Reverend Brewster during one of his beloved Proverbs. Sensing no imminent end to the reading, she was forthright and direct.

"Reverend, we are here about our...about our *marriage*." Brewster stopped the reading abruptly. He conveyed no sense of surprise or disappointment, as marital counseling was certainly one of the most common activities of his ministry. He felt this would be one of those times in which no additional prodding was required. He merely looked up from his worn King James Bible and patiently waited for her to continue. Joshua looked like he was ready to crawl under the floorboards.

"I'm sorry to be abrupt, but I'm not sure if our marriage is...healthy. If...WE are healthy."

"Mary, you both have been the picture of health. Has some wickedness befallen your home?"

"It's just that...I worry my betrothed is not fulfilling his husbandly duties."

"His duties? Mary, your home is splendid. Joshua's barrels are magnificent and I have no doubt there is food on the table. I know he leads a Godly life in a Godly home. What is he not fulfilling?" Mary's eyes fell to her lap and Brewster knew instantly where the conversation was going.

"It's just that…well…eight months, Reverend Brewster. Eight Months! Our hours of work and labor are very happy and wholesome but…shouldn't I be with child after this time?"

Brewster sighed, once again louder than he had hoped. The situation was a common lament in the colony. "Joshua, you've been as silent as the desert. Speak freely and openly."

Joshua sat quietly with his head low and was barely audible when he spoke. "I guess I'm exhausted, Reverend." Brewster sat patiently, confident the young man was freely confiding. "The work, it is never done as you no doubt know. The barrels are endless, constantly needing built, rebuilt, patched and sold. The fences throughout Middleborough need mending, and it seems the wages are so scant. And we both had such a difficult winter, rife with maladies of coughing and fever. But Mary is…" The young man's voice buckled and Brewster wondered if he would shed a tear. "Mary is such a delight, Reverend. Every day I thank the Almighty we are alive and we are together."

"Joshua, I understand completely, and do not feel alone in this situation. We are a blessed people in a covenant with the Lord to bring civilization and the light of Christ to this wilderness, and though our spirit is strong, are bodies are often numb with fatigue. And Mary, I counsel patience and understanding, as you have a loving husband and the situation is no fault of yours.

"Here is my counsel for the situation. Firstly, as always, a steady regimen of prayer. Pray daily for each other, pray for health, and pray you may be fruitful and multiply. Secondly, in the ensuing months, I want all labors to terminate by sunset. I'm sure the barrels and fences will still be there in the morning. Thirdly, I recommend scripture in the evening."

"Scripture, Reverend?" Mary conveyed a sense of doubt but her trust in her pastor's judgement was absolute.

"Yes. I want you to read the Song of Solomon aloud to

one another. It is a love poem reminding us that the intimacy between a husband and wife is one of our greatest gifts. *Let him kiss me with the kisses of his mouth: for thy love is better than wine.* It is, umm…most stimulating.

"And finally, come see me later next week, Joshua. The Narragansett healers speak highly of an herb that can be used for cooking that is allegedly quite efficacious in these matters. Summer Savory I believe it is called. I will procure some and want to see you spice your meals with it in the ensuing weeks. Yes, I believe we have a satisfactory course of action. Do not be troubled, you were very wise to seek counsel on this matter. I have no doubt by this time next year we will have a strapping young blessing in your home."

After a brief prayer, the young Farwells took their leave, with Joshua leading the way at a rapid clip. Brewster sighed deeply and paced the floor, rifling his hand through his dark mane of hair. The hour was growing late and he did not anticipate any additional callers. He sat down to refresh himself with a smattering of cheese and another mug of small beer.

Brewster was in a weary state and restlessly contemplative. Marital counseling was growing increasingly difficult since he bid farewell to his beloved. What he would give to hold her hand one more time, to read one more love sonnet together, to share a glass of wine. Soon he was standing by the bookshelf, pondering a sonnet to lull himself to slumber, but instead fell upon his cherished *Institutes of the Christian Religion* by John Calvin.

He turned to the cover page as he had done so many times before and read the inscription, signifying the book was a gift from his grandfather, Elder William Brewster of Duxbury. He was merely an infant when the gift was bestowed, and had scarcely a memory of his famous relative, as he met his eternal reward when young Israel Brewster was two. *"The fear of the LORD is the beginning of knowledge, but fools despise wisdom and instruction."* The inscription was fading over the decades, but he would never forget from whose hand it came.

Elder William Brewster. Israel Brewster, like many of his era, revered his parents and grandparents with a sense of profound awe. Israel could scarcely imagine the divinely-inspired fortitude and self-sacrifice that culminated in a two-month journey across the treacherous Atlantic Ocean to a strange and brutal wilderness.

Israel often envisioned Elder Brewster providing spiritual guidance and solemn confidence amidst the terror and carnage inherent in the journey and subsequent years. Every time Israel opened this precious volume of Calvin, he wondered forlornly what his ancestors would think of him and his ministry. Would they scoff and leer at the luxuries and bountiful food surrounding him here in Middleborough? Brewster could scarcely remember the last time he was genuinely hungry due to lack of food. William Brewster was building the foundation of a holy new world, a historical vision sanctioned by the Almighty. And his grandson? He was spending his days lugging timber, counseling newlyweds too exhausted to be amorous, and fighting the battles of Satanically felled cows.

When troubles and self-doubt came, Israel was often comforted by the writings of Calvin, one of the foundations on which his life, and the lives of the colonists was built. He had scarcely completed his seventh page, when, after rubbing his fatigued eyes, he noticed his correspondence on a small shelf in the corner of the desk.

Brewster gently chided himself as he had become woefully behind in his correspondence, guiltily grabbed the stack of letters, and mentally plotted a cursory response to each. There were letters from distant relatives in the mother country. They were now ten years into the restoration of the monarchy, and his staunchly Puritan cousins had resigned themselves to the situation after decades of tumult.

Other letters appeared routine, but well received. He looked forward to a missive from his friend and ally, Reverend John Eliot. Certainly no one in the new world was as passionate and devout about bringing the Word to the natives. Approximately eight years ago, Eliot had translated the Bible into the Massachutt language, and it served as a priceless resource for Brewster during his missionary work. Other pieces of correspondence he recognized from friends and family in Plimoth. The passing of his beloved had generated a remarkable outpouring of condolences and sympathy, and he was surprised and pleased the written exchanges remained frequent, although many were devolving into thinly-veiled matchmaking schemes.

He was perusing a proposed introduction to a prosperous merchant's second cousin in Dorchester when, from the corner of his eye, he noted a remarkable thing. A letter from the Second Church in Boston. Tearing open the letter, he was stunned and delighted that the Reverend Increase Mather, perhaps the most influential scholar in the new world, had directed a letter to him. He had scarcely finished the introduction when there was a timid knock at his door.

Setting aside the letter, Brewster rubbed his eyes and answered the call. No one had previously scheduled time for counseling, but frequently it was the unannounced visits that yielded the most spiritual fruit. A second knock resounded through the room, more forceful than the first and Brewster opened the door and was greeted by the widow, Martha Leister.

"Forgive me Reverend, I know the hour is late and I am unannounced."

"Nonsense, Mrs. Leister. My home is always open." It was evident Martha Leister had spent the better part of the evening in a state of tears. Mrs. Leister, age thirty-six, was a plump and ruddy woman who suffered the gravest of travesties three months ago when she lost her husband Bartholomew and their nine-year old son Peter during a hunting trip in which they both became disoriented in a blizzard and perished. Peter had been her only child. "Can I fetch you anything? Some cheese perhaps?"

"You are always kind, Reverend and I do dislike calling on you so. It's just…" Mrs. Leister was unable to finish her thoughts as her voice drifted away into anguished silence. These could be some of the most rewarding moments to a young clergyman, but also the most challenging.

"How I hate to keep coming to you, with you and all of your own grief. But when? When Reverend? When is daybreak? Will the torment never end?"

As usual Reverend Brewster called on scripture, and called on the passage from second Corinthians that he had recited and prayed upon so much in the last year the words were as familiar to him as his name.

"Blessed be God, even the Father of our Lord Jesus Christ, the Father of mercies, and the God of all comfort; Who comforteth us in all our tribulation, that we may be able to comfort them which are in any trouble, by the comfort wherewith we ourselves are comforted of God. For as the sufferings of Christ abound in us, so our consolation also aboundeth by Christ."

Mrs. Leister nodded politely but no tears had subsided. "But what about YOU, Reverend Brewster? How do you overcome your grief so handily? Who do you rely upon when the pain feels as a mania?" Brewster struggled for a heartfelt reply but remained silent. "Do you ever wonder, Reverend? Wonder about…" She left the sentence unfinished as she reached for Calvin's volume, still open on Brewster's desk. He may have chided another for so presumptuously accosting one of his cherished possessions, but certainly not Mrs. Leister. She peered at the book through moist eyes and then back at him, as if the presence of the book was adequate to formulate the question.

"Do I wonder...about what, Mrs. Leister?"

"About the Almighty. And suffering. Our destinies, Reverend. Was Bartholomew predestined to die? What manner of wickedness have I manifest, so that Peter should suffer so?" She had regained her composure remarkably well. Brewster knew Martha Leister, as the eldest child of a clergyman and separatist scholar, was one of the most educated and well-read ladies in either Plimoth or the Massachusetts Bay colony. Like her father, she was well versed in the great scholars like Calvin, Luther, and Zwingli. Brewster leaned forward to listen carefully but the exhaustion generated by the day's labors was now pressing heavily upon him. She continued with no interjection from him.

"Was I not pleasing to the Almighty in manner of thought and deed? Have you examined your own conduct justly?" Brewster could not mask the pain and emotion this last comment elicited but continued to remain silent. "Reverend Brewster, I am aged thirty-six years. Thirty-six! And I am not certain I am any closer to blessed assurance than the day of my baptism. Forgive me, I know my words are wrought with controversy and are difficult to hear. But how can I be forever confident I am a saint? How can I know God has chosen me among the elect?"

"Mrs. Leister, I realize these last months have been a torment. Please know that God will give you the strength to persevere. Are you studying the book of Job?"

"Yes, I have read it three times but it is failing to provide solace. Or I suppose, the failure is mine. The failure to derive solace."

"Mrs. Leister, I pray you may find solace in the weeks and months ahead. You have my deepest sympathies and I know these tortures shall pass. As you pray and examine your life, your blessed assurance will materialize. It may be tonight, it may be next month, it may be on your death bed but you will come to accept your role as a saint and the elect of God. You are an esteemed member of this holy community and I assure you your life and actions are most pleasing to the Almighty. May we read from the book of James?"

"But Luther attested…"

"I am aware of Martin Luther's thoughts on the book of James, Mrs. Leister. But very well. Let us go the words of our Savior." He took her hand and read slowly and quietly from the Gospel of Mark.

"And Jesus answering saith unto them, Have faith in God. For verily I say unto you, That whosoever shall say unto this mountain, Be thou removed, and be thou cast into the sea; and shall not doubt in his heart, but shall believe that those things which he saith shall come to pass; he shall have whatsoever he saith. Therefore I say unto you, What things so ever ye desire, when ye pray, believe that ye receive them, and ye shall have them."

"Good night, Reverend Brewster. And may the peace of the Lord be yours."

CHAPTER FIVE

ENROUTE TO BOSTON

Israel Brewster awoke in a state of numb exhaustion. He was exhausted physically, emotionally, and spiritually. He had dreamt no dreams and had achieved no rest. This was the day the Lord had made, however, and the Reverend Brewster would be glad in it.

Morning prayer focused on the counseling of the previous evening. He prayed for strong marriages. He prayed for the continued prosperity of Josiah Franklin's farm. He implored the Almighty to cast hope and faith across Mrs. Leister's painful grief. And he sought strength and wisdom, so he could continue to serve the community as the Lord commanded.

Strength and wisdom were the themes of morning scripture. He turned to the New Testament and the book of James (knowing he would be free of any Mrs. Leister's Lutheresque reprimands).

"If any of you lack wisdom, let him ask of God, that giveth to all liberally, and upbraideth not; and it shall be given him."

And two chapters later:

"But the wisdom that is from above is first pure, then peaceable, gentle, easy to be intreated, full of mercy and good fruits, without partiality, and without hypocrisy."

Brewster had no formal commitments scheduled today, and he envisioned a day of scripture and correspondence. Correspondence. He had scarcely scratched the surface of his correspondence when Mrs. Leister arrived last night, and he had left it untended. And the letter! Brewster was stunned that he could forget he had a letter from Reverend Mather of Boston.

Reverend Increase Mather was one of, if not the most influential scholar and clergyman in all of New England. He had been serving as chief clergy of the illustrious Second Church in the north end of Boston for seven years now. Few in the colonies could compete with his fervor, formal education, and intellectual acumen. Brewster feverishly grasped the letter.

May 9, 1671
Reverend Increase Mather, Boston

To Reverend Israel Brewster, my esteemed brother in Christ

I hope this missive finds you and the disciples of Middleborough well and at peace. At the risk of presumption, I have taken it upon myself to cast introductions and cordial tidings amongst the young clergy of Plimoth and Massachusetts Bay for purposes of mentorship and spiritual solidarity.
Difficult days are amongst us and I pray our brothers and sisters may remain strong in faith and worthy of the gifts bestowed upon us from the Almighty's bounty. I am most anxious to meet with you in order to solidify the bonds of friendship, and to assess the spiritual health of the congregation. My travels, God willing, shall be minimal this spring, and rest assured you will find me at work at or near the meeting house in the north square most any day. Your visitation would be most welcome, and I pray your journey fruitful and safe.

Yours in Christ
Increase Mather

Brewster read the letter three times to ensure he had not missed any veiled instructions or subtle nuances. Increase Mather! The Reverend Mather, scholar of Harvard and the prestigious Trinity College of Dublin, was summoning him, the humble Israel Brewster of Middleborough. He was almost too stunned to move.

Since the letter was addressed over two weeks ago, and there was no value in keeping the Reverend Mather waiting, Brewster made plans to leave immediately. He quickly devoured a modest breakfast and lingered a bit in his grooming rituals. He donned his most elegant coat and hat, and contemplated what if anything he should bring from his library. He quickly scoffed at such a pointless endeavor, as certainly Mather's library, both mental and physical, would exceed his own by levels of magnitude.

Brewster made the required rounds through Middleborough, announcing his plans while doing his best not to sound boastful (*"The Reverend Mather has requested my counsel at the Second Church…I have been summoned for prayerful deliberations…I am journeying to Boston for worship and camaraderie"*) but most everything sounded pretentious and ill-mannered. He procured a horse, which was a three-year brown mare, he gathered letters to be delivered, and he took countless requests for dry goods.

The sun was now two hours old, and Brewster anticipated a twelve-hour ride to Boston with a planned slumber in Weymouth. He hurried through his farewells, and with minimal fanfare was on his way.

This would only be Brewster's second sojourn to Boston in all of his days, and he did his best to contain his giddy excitement. He was soon engrossed in psalmody, and as he left the outskirts of Middleborough, he grew louder and more boisterous as the potential to be overheard subsided. His voice rang out across the countryside on that pleasant spring morning, much to the increasing consternation of the mare, whom, as Brewster was previously informed, was saddled with the sadly uncreative moniker of "Brownie."

Two hours later the sun was rising higher in the May sky, and Brewster was pleased with his progress. He anticipated arriving in Bridgewater before mid-afternoon and would procure water and nutrition for Brownie.

While most colonists dreaded the tedium and loneliness of long journeys by horseback, Brewster, as with so many other undertakings, seemed to relish it, and he approached it with his usual sense of gratitude and enthusiasm. He enjoyed the solitude and the opportunity to commune with nature and the Almighty. During these prolonged periods of uninterrupted contemplation, Brewster's mind often returned to conversations or events from years past, things that simply refused to fade with the relentless march of time.

"You have offered me much but I have accepted nothing. You have seen this with your own eyes. Though my destiny is closed, my fault is with the heavens. I have not been corrupted...no...mackiki... by the English. Ensure the people understand and bear no ill tidings."

Brewster often marveled at the dialogue and conversations from distant years he could recall verbatim. His memory was a gift from heaven, and his knowledge of scripture was usually without peer.

He vigorously shook his head in an effort to rouse himself from the past, and he recommitted himself to the present. He was certain there would be much to discuss with Reverend Mather, and he would need to keep focused on the long journey.

Reverend Increase Mather. Even his name was so impressive and so unique. Brewster had heard second-hand that "Increase" was ascribed to *"permanent increase, of all manner, where God favored the people with the nativity."* Others told him it was a literal translation of the Biblical "Yosef." Brewster wondered if he would appear provincial and uninformed if he inquired about it while visiting.

Relations with Plimoth and Massachusetts Bay had been very good these last few decades, but Brewster recalled tales from the elders of Plimoth about the earliest days. A mere ten years after Brewster's grandfather made shore with Bradford, Standish, and the other pilgrims of Christ, Winthrop arrived with 700 colonists and settled less than fifty miles to the north. Although holy and dedicated to scripture, these new colonists often astounded Plimoth with their hope and belief in a reformed English church. Their gullibility was deplorable, as the Church of England had clearly wasted away into a bloated, unholy menagerie of corruption and decadence.

Winthrop had always been concerned his followers would be influenced by the separatism of Brewster's forbears (the only rational doctrine) and that certainly transpired. The men of Massachusetts Bay were more worldly; they were better educated with more impressive status and wealth. Brewster recalled William Bradford's vocation was a cloth-worker, whereas Winthrop was a silver-tongued barrister, working at the behest of the English government itself. The men of Massachusetts Bay were at times haughty and arrogant, strangely lacking in Christian humility. Brewster recalled the tale his uncle, Jonathan Brewster, loved to tell.

"Back in 1635 there were members of a Massachusetts Bay congregation in Dorchester. Out of the blue, they opted to move near the Connecticut River. I was operating a trading post in Windsor for Plimoth colony. I showed them Christian hospitality, and helped them procure canoes and guides so they could explore the region. The Dorchester men, much to my shock, announced they would be taking over the land and building settlements on it.

"I did, in a polite Christian fashion, point out that Plimoth had purchased the land from the natives to establish a fur trade, and that there were thousands of other acres available. But the Dorchester men, exhibiting their Massachusetts Bay arrogance, would not be deterred and attested they were only doing the will of God.

"Subsequently two boatloads of Dorchester settlers left Boston for the Connecticut post. Their boats were wrecked on Brown's Island in Plimoth Bay. The Plimoth men came to their aid and gathered the victims and their soggy possessions.

Astoundingly, a third boat that was carrying cargo for the settlers was blown ashore off Sandwich. Yet again, the Christian people of Plimoth rescued the goods and turned them over to the owners.

"Eventually the Dorchester men felt shame and embarrassment at their lack of virtue and at the Godliness of the Plimoth men. Praise to the Almighty, for they contemplated their ill ways, and decided to forego their claim on the land lawfully purchased by Plimoth, and to move on."

Brewster continued to pass the hours with more psalmody. The countryside was lovely, and he was entranced. He sang loudly and enthusiastically.

"O worship the LORD in the beauty of holiness: fear before him, all the earth.

Say among the heathen that the LORD reigneth: the world also shall be established that it shall not be moved: he shall judge the people righteously.

Let the heavens rejoice, and let the earth be glad; let the sea roar, and the fullness thereof.

Let the field be joyful, and all that is therein: then shall all the trees of the wood rejoice."

Brewster reached such a feverish crescendo singing the glories of the fields and trees that even Brownie had to convey her displeasure, and she snorted derisively. Brewster had a good chuckle and was pleased that they were approaching the outskirts of Bridgewater.

He whiled away a pleasant afternoon hour in the small hamlet. Brownie was pleased with her offerings of oats and water, and Brewster enjoyed a large helping of venison and onions washed down with a remarkably good small beer. Although fresh, clean water was much more accessible and plentiful in the new world compared to the densely populated cities of the mother country and Europe, the colonists still reveled in the soothing, nutritious quality of beer with minimally intoxicating qualities. For certainly the first book of Timothy was wise:

> *"Drink no longer water, but use a little wine for thy stomach's sake and thine often infirmities."*

    Being as there didn't seem to be any wine in Bridgewater (save for the precious batch reserved for Holy Communion), Brewster could not resist a third helping of Bridgewater's superb local offering. He dined with two carpenters who had been fabricating furniture all day and were most anxious to be regaled with news of Middleborough. They inquired numerous times about unsettling tales of witchcraft lurking amidst their southern neighbor and seemed disappointed when Brewster conveyed that the holy work of the Lord continues unabated in Middleborough with no evidence of infiltration by Satan's minions.
    The young reverend attempted to redirect the conversation to his genuine interest, the steps and procedures required to fabricate the intricate oak desk they were discussing. Brewster was also curious of their thoughts regarding two of the most renowned craftsmen in the colonies, Searle and Dennis. He was aware these two underwent their formal training in England, and relocated to Ipswich a few years ago. Despite the limitations inherent in New England, they continued to craft furniture with no decrease in quality or ornamentation. They were known for their distinctive elaborate carving, and their ostentation was a source of debate among the faithful. Some claimed the works of Searle and Dennis bordered on popish extravagance and frippery, but Brewster did not know

any wife in the colony who did not crave one of their famed lift-top chests.

The carpenters, Jonathan and Isaiah, had been immersed in furniture for far too long and had no wish to discuss it any further during their repose. They were intent on their probing discussions of witchcraft, specifically, if as a formally trained clergyman, Brewster had any guidance on how to distinguish the devil's kiss versus routine skin maladies. They were familiar with the third nipple (as was even the most uninformed citizen), but they craved additional insights. Had Brewster personally identified and sentenced any witches?

The memory of Winthrop sentencing the witch Margaret Jones to die in Charlestown seemed so recent in the colony, but it was more than twenty years ago. A mere two years later, Alice Lake was executed near Boston, but Brewster had his doubts if she was a witch or merely a lost sinner. Regardless, many in the colony agreed nowadays that the battle against witchcraft had fallen far too dormant, and Satan was undoubtedly capitalizing on their lack of vigilance.

Brewster realized daylight was a finite resource in New England, even in May. He extended cordial tidings, made good on the required compensation for his victuals, and bade the town farewell. He and Brownie, equally pleased with the hospitality of Bridgewater, resumed their northern trek. The sun was sinking in the sky and Brewster remained silent. He was thankful for the solitude, as a midday meal rife with onions and beer had rendered him so flatulent even Brownie seemed to take offense, and Brownie had no right to complain.

Brewster was reminiscing about his youth and fondly recalling his service in the militia. Even as a young man his vision was marginal, and a dairy barn would have nothing to fear from his loaded and pointed musket. Still, as always, Brewster overcame any shortcomings in natural talent with his Calvinist work ethic and his joyful enthusiasm, and he was a serviceable militiaman. He began recalling the bawdy songs he and his company would sing during the ceaseless hours of frigid boredom, and soon field and farm echoed with a joyful noise.

> *"In Amsterdam there lived a maid*
> *Mark you well what I say!*
> *In Amsterdam there lives a maid,*
> *And this fair maid my trust betrayed.*
> *I'll go no more a rovin, with you fair maid.*
> *A roving, A roving, since roving's been my ru-i-in,*
> *I'll go no more a roving, with you fair maid."*

Brewster's nervous eyes darted forward and behind. During these seven hours he encountered surprisingly few travelers, mostly merchants and peddlers bringing their wares south from Boston. He had no desire to be overheard and embarrassed by his tawdry ditty.

> *"Her eyes are like two stars so bright,*
> *Mark you well what I say*
> *Her eyes are like two stars so bright,*
> *Her face is fair, her step is light.*
> *I asked this fair maid to take a walk,*
> *Mark well what I do say*
> *I asked this maid out for a walk*
> *That we might have some private talk.*
> *Then I took this fair maid's lily white hand,*
> *Mark well what I do say*
> *I took this fair maid's lily white hand*

In mine as we walked along the strand.
Then I put my arm around her waist
Mark well what I do say!
For I put my arm around her waist
And from her lips snatched a kiss in haste!"

Brewster actually giggled he was feeling so giddy. He struggled to recall the entire song.

"Then a great big Dutchman rammed my bow
Mark well what I do say
For a great big Dutchman rammed my bow,
And said, "Young man, dis bin MEIN frau!"
Then take warning boys, from me,
Mark well what I do say!
So take a warning, boys, from me,
With other men's wives don't make too free.
For if you do you will surely rue
Mark well what I do say!
For if you do you will surely rue
Your act, and find my words come true."

As the sun grew lower, Brewster grew more earnest and somber. Although the ditty was fun, adultery was serious indeed and he was thankful it was not tolerated amidst the saints of the New World. Brewster's mind drifted, and he tried to recollect the sermons he personally delivered on the grave sin. He contemplated the ceaseless vigilance of the community, the numerous tribunals of inquiry he took part in over the years, and most of all, he ruminated on the intense punishment the condemned faced. The justice of the Lord was indeed fair and true.

The hours passed quickly and Brownie's pace seemed to slow accordingly. Weymouth beckoned in the distance, and Brewster would need to arrange for a meal and lodging. He had no doubt he would be well provided for, and he looked forward to the Christian charity of Weymouth.

Weymouth was quiet as the sun set on this lovely Tuesday. The streets were practically vacant and he was blessed to meet with a shopkeeper closing his doors for the evening. After brief introductions, Brewster explained his situation and the shopkeeper, Elias Parsons, apologized that Reverend Brewster would be most uncomfortable at his homestead, as Mr. and Mrs. Parsons could scarcely find their own slumber with six rambunctious children in their midst. He directed Brewster to the Billington farm on the outskirts of town. Benjamin and Clara Billington had just bid their two youngest children farewell, as they had gone to sea to make their name and fortune, and Parsons was confident Brewster would be a welcome guest. Brewster uttered his gratitude, and conveyed his joy and admiration that the Lord had blessed Parsons with six healthy children. Within minutes he found the Billington farm.

Fortuitously, Benjamin and Clara Billington had just put a supper of roast pork and beans on the table, and providing nourishment to a traveler, in addition to being their Christian duty, was a pleasant surprise. Strangers were a rarity in Weymouth, and hosting a clergyman as young and high-spirited as Brewster was a noteworthy and welcome event.

Brewster relished the new friendship and sought to know all he could of their family. The Billingtons were blessed with four children. Their eldest daughter, Eleanor, had married a trader and was residing in New Haven while expecting her first child. Their second child, Thomas, had perished long ago from smallpox before his tenth birthday. The twins, Jeremiah and

Joshua, now eighteen years of age, were on a fishing voyage aboard a boat recently built at the new shipyard at Chebacco Point. Mrs. Billington said she prayed every day for the safety of her boys and for plentiful fish.

    Brewster had genuinely forgotten how fatigued he felt that morning, and needless to say his faculties were strained. When Mrs. Billington ascertained that the dashing young reverend was a childless widower, Brewster thought he could clearly detect her feminine mind manufacturing a whirlwind of romantic matchmaking scenarios with nieces, daughters of neighboring farms, or cousins from England. Brewster remained politely aloof regarding her machinations and felt relieved she did not push the issue.

    Brewster also noticed that while the Billingtons were delighted to regale him with anecdotes regarding the farm and their children, they appeared quite aloof regarding their own history in the colony. This came as no surprise to Brewster, as there were few if any secrets between the colonists of New England, and anyone slightly versed in the history of the colony would recognize the name Billington as one of infamy.

    The tale of the Billington clan was indeed remarkable, and Brewster strained to recollect the stories his father passed down from his father. If memory served, the first transgression was aboard the Mayflower with a young Billington child. His name was Francis. After arriving in Plimoth Harbor and still onboard the Mayflower, the child somehow took hold of his father's musket and shot it off inside the ship. The result was a shower of sparks around an open barrel of gunpowder. Some say he almost blew up the Mayflower, but Brewster suspected that was an exaggeration.

Brewster could also recall a separate incident in which John Billington was brought before the authorities and charged with insubordination, but he was pardoned after a profound apology and avoided punishment. Shortly thereafter, his son John wandered off and was taken by local natives. The colony had to send out a party to retrieve the boy. Brewster could also recall that allegedly Billington was involved in additional scandal, a failed revolt of some sort against the Plimoth church—but he claimed ignorance and once again avoided punishment.

Brewster did his best not to appear distracted and rude at the table, but the more he recalled of the Plimoth Billingtons, the more astounded he was. Everyone in the colony knew that in 1630 John Billington shot and killed John Newcomen over an old quarrel of some sort. Billington was put on trial and hung until dead. Even Billington's wife besmirched the family's good name. She was guilty of a slander offense and was placed in the stocks and whipped. Perhaps his host Benjamin Billington was completely unrelated to that problematic clan, but Brewster assumed that any inquiries on the topic would be most unwelcome.

After dinner and a brief reading of scripture, Brewster was shown to a very comfortable room and slept deeply. He could almost feel the "clip-clop" gait of Brownie in his dreams. He awoke well after dawn, however, drenched with sweat and palpitations. Before he startled awake he could see her in the small room. He could see her face, he could see her brown eyes and he was cradling the child. Her voice was tender and weak.

"How blessed I have been."

Brewster leapt from the bed trying to distance

himself from his nighttime torment. He washed his face vigorously. His hosts had already arisen and Brewster surmised they were out on the farm commencing the day's labors. He felt a torrent of restless energy and was delighted to stumble upon a goodly amount of wood still to be split. He reveled in the opportunity to repay the Billingtons' hospitality in some small way, and he chopped wood fervently for at least an hour until the Billingtons returned. They were most grateful for his efforts, and after cordial farewells and prayers for their family, he was sent on his way with a loaf of bread and a jug of milk.

Brownie also appeared invigorated and they found their way back to the road for the five-hour journey to the "city upon a hill." He knew from a previous visit it was actually a city upon three hills, but he did not begrudge Winthrop.

Brewster was once again blessed with marvelous weather, and the morning was glorious. He was soon traversing "the neck" and he shuddered with a feeling of dread. Unlike many in the colony, Israel Brewster was aware that Mary Dyer, the heretic Quaker, was hung from an elm tree at the neck of Boston, and not Boston Common as frequently believed. Brewster could not wait to get through it.

He was soon met at the city gate. It was difficult not to feel a sense of jealousy at the protection the unique geography afforded the city. He identified himself to the sentries as a clergyman on church business and was soon inside the grand city.

The sights and sounds of the city were marvelous. The population, since the day Winthrop led 700 devout followers ashore, had exploded to at least 4,000 people in a mere 40 years. Brewster was travelling north on High Street and could see the

Boston Common to his left. To his immediate right was the fort on Fort Hill. He continued on the main thoroughfare through town and was soon in the heart of Boston, with the market and a meetinghouse all within view.

Brewster tarried to marvel at the boats and activity at the town dock just east of the market. The noise and the bustle seemed overwhelming, and even Brownie seemed to become slightly agitated. Brewster saw yet another sight that made him shudder. In addition to the rope, nails, lumber and molasses being staged on the wharf, Brewster witnessed six or seven African men marched in chains from a trading ship.

He proceeded in a northeast direction along Hanover Street into the north end and could see the modest "Mill Hill" in the distance with the windmill perched mightily atop. He was soon in North Square and in the presence of the Second Church of Boston.

Although he was impressed with the size of the meeting house, he felt slightly underwhelmed. In the back of his mind he had hopes for a European-style cathedral, but he quickly denounced himself for such foolery in Puritan Boston. The structure was grand, however. He was tempted to seek nourishment before presenting himself, but the milk and bread the Billingtons provided had proven most hearty.

After hastily securing Brownie, he made his appearance. He assumed the grand Reverend Mather would certainly be engaged in some remarkable business elsewhere on behalf of the faithful, so he was surprised and elated when a burly parishioner, immersed in the repair of a troublesome stretch of railing, directed him to the vestry.

After three resolute knocks on Mather's mighty oak door, Brewster was standing before the gentleman himself. The first thing that struck him was Increase Mather was remarkably handsome. It was difficult to gauge his eyes in the limited light of the vestry, but Mather had soft, attentive brown eyes that framed a prominent, slightly aquiline nose. He was blessed with a remarkable head of hair that obviated the need for a wig, and his locks of curls cascaded past his collar. While most men of New England, after a life of living and working in the elements possessed rugged, often pock-marked and ruddy complexions, Mather's was aristocratic and delicate. Finally, he was stunned by how young he was. Brewster would have almost described him as borderline effeminate until his voice boomed through the room with an aura of leadership and authority.

"Yes, friend? How many I be of service on this glorious day?" Brewster almost stuttered. "Reverend Mather? I am Reverend Israel Brewster of Middleborough. I was pleased to receive your invitation and I have made the journey."

"Brewster…Brewster. I am afraid I am not familiar. No, clearly there has been some error or mischievous prank at work here. I do apologize for the inconvenience, but if you could take your leave now I am quite busy. Good day."

Brewster stood in stunned silence and tried to think of the most graceful way to extricate himself from this humiliation. "Well…I am sorry, but I…the letter…I'm not sure." He failed to convey a cogent thought before the room erupted with boisterous laughter.

"My dear Brewster, forgive my merriment. Oh, I am childish at times. We must, however, vanquish that youthful gullibility. There is much afoot. Come, come and sit. Tell me of your journey."

Brewster lit up with amazement that the illustrious Mather could be capable of a prank. Soon he had sent for tea, and Brewster tried to recall the last time he was treated to tea from a genuine English tea service.

They discussed his journey, the merits of Brownie (which Brewster found to be increasingly limited), and observations of Weymouth and Bridgewater. Mather was pleased to hear of the carpenters and their vigilance regarding witchcraft. They spent a great deal of time discussing Brewster's famous grandfather, and Mather regaled him with numerous anecdotes about England, Ireland, and his time as a chaplain during the civil war.

Brewster took in the sumptuous vestry and the library before him. Zwingli. Calvin. Luther. Bullinger. Knox. He could not wait to confer with this colossus of the faith. One of the tomes, however, he did not recognize: *The Mystery of Israel's Salvation*. After inquiring, Brewster discovered Mather had completed it less than two years ago.

Mather was aware of Brewster's recent tragedy and he offered his condolences. His advice was heartfelt but somewhat predictable. "Faith, prayer and scripture, Reverend. Remember the second chapter of Genesis, verse eighteen. I am certain it does not need reciting." Brewster assured him it did not, and the conversation evolved to matters at hand.

"Well, Reverend, I do appreciate this journey you have made. Horseback from Middleborough is no small feat. In these trying times I have found it incumbent upon myself to make every effort to meet, confer with, and dare I say, mentor the clergy throughout the colony. I have been back in New England for ten years now and I confess I am increasingly fearful for the fate of our endeavor, the English Israel, for I know that God is just and will not abide disobedience." Mather paused then continued.

"I must confess, Reverend Brewster, that I have been naive in decades past. Sometimes I wonder if I have faithfully adhered to the path the Almighty has chosen for me." Brewster could not help noticing that, although Mather couldn't be more than five years older than he was, he conducted himself with an air of a grand elder. "Reverend Brewster, how old were you during the restoration?"

Mather was referring to the dreaded event in 1660, when Oliver Cromwell's Puritan government had run its course, and the citizenry lost faith in his heir, Richard. A monarch was placed back on the throne, and Puritans on both side of the Atlantic bemoaned the reversal, as Anglicanism was restored to its previous prominence. Mather promptly left England and returned to Boston.

"Umm...seventeen years I believe?" Brewster was still momentarily perplexed by the phrase "English Israel", confusing one of Mather's favorite descriptions of their divinely sanctioned society with his own given name. "I would have been absorbed in militia duty."

"Indeed, Reverend, indeed. At the time I was disillusioned and perplexed by the will of the Almighty, and how so much was sacrificed and victory was so fleeting. Once Cromwell's protectorate had been sanctified, we all wondered about the fate and dare I say, even the *need* for Massachusetts Bay colony. Still, it reinforced my destiny. This noble undertaking of ours is the only course, the only means in which the elect can remain holy in the eyes of the Lord and build a righteous society. But since my return, I fear much sin has insidiously manifest itself. I fear comfort and soft living is omnipresent, and we are lacking the courage and conviction of our parents and grandparents." Brewster politely nodded his assent and Mather continued.

"Are you familiar with liquid molasses, Reverend? It goes by many names. Rumbullion, Kill-Divil, Barbados liquor. Now drink is in itself a good creature of God, but the abuse of drink is from Satan, and this intoxicating concoction is indeed from the hand of the evil one. And do you know where you might find the most recent distillery in the new world, the newest venture designed to trade drunken misery and squalor for profit? Three hundred yards from where you're enjoying your tea, Reverend. In this city, the brightest light of the English Israel, we are selling rum for profit!"

Brewster felt that he was obliged to speak. "Drunkenness, I'm afraid, is still a malady afflicting Middleborough. And among the Wampanoag…"

"It is a disgrace and an abomination. Charged with our sacred duty to bring the light to the heathen and what course do we take? Poisoning them with the vilest of concoctions so we can line our pockets at their expense. And I am sure you're aware how poorly the heathen mix with alcohol." Brewster again nodded his assent.

"And what of our sinful nature? Working on the Sabbath, lustful adultery, more and more popish frippery. I fear God's chosen people shall be humbled again. Tell me Reverend, what was the divine instrument of the Almighty's holy wrath when the Kingdom of Israel was wrought with wickedness and idolatry?" Brewster opened his mouth to answer, and quickly realized there was no need. "Savages, of course. Unholy, vicious savages. The Assyrians. Do you recall who led the victory?" Once again, Brewster needlessly tried to utter a syllable. "Sargon of course. Sargon the second I believe. And did the Kingdom of Judah take heed? Nay, they resumed their sinful rebellion against God's word despite the righteousness of the prophets. Somehow Brewster got a word in.

"Zephaniah. The prophet. He testified to King Josiah, *On the day of the LORD's wrath, in the fire of his passion, the whole land shall be consumed.*"

Mather appeared stunned and simultaneously delighted. "Excellent, Reverend. And how was Judah consumed? Earthquakes? Locusts? Volcanoes?"

Brewster promptly replied, "the warriors of the ungodly. King Nebuchadnezzar broke through Jerusalem's walls, conquering the city. King Zedekiah was captured and blinded. After his sons were killed, he was marched off to exile."

Mather was transfixed. "And tell me Reverend? What will be the instrument of the Almighty's wrath among his chosen people in this new world? We have survived blizzards, and starvation, and disease. What, then, shall befall us?" Brewster remained silent and reached for his tea. "The savages, Reverend. Wampanoag. Narragansett. Nipmunk. The Pequot wars were just a warning from the Almighty, and I fear greater wrath is to come."

Brewster loathed muttering a contrary syllable to the colossus of the New World, but he could not share in Mather's jeremiad. "Your words are indeed stirring, Reverend Mather. But I am pleased with the progress we are making in Middleborough with God's help. Reverend Eliot's efforts have been remarkable throughout the colony, and I will be leading missionary services next week. I am concerned with the rising worldliness and sinful nature of our countrymen, but I trust in Providence that more and more natives will be brought into the light."

"Your efforts are commendable and our resident apostle to the heathen, Reverend Eliot, will be glorified throughout the ages. Under no circumstances are we to tire or fail in our sacredly sanctioned duty to these unenlightened." Mather leaned forward.

"But make no mistake, Reverend. The will of the Almighty is present in every aspect of our daily lives. We pride ourselves as the predestined elect of the Lord, but the Lord's elect would naturally be averse to the sin and wickedness permeating these colonies. Are you active in the General Court at Plimoth, Reverend?" Brewster confessed he was not, and Mather continued.

"I know the ways of Plimoth men are different than their brothers to the north, but I implore you to partake in the public affairs and civic judgments of your government. You are clearly one of the most level, learned young men in the colony and these dangerous times demand leadership. If I'm not mistaken, the General Court convenes in a special session this Friday."

That was the day after tomorrow.

CHAPTER SIX
PLIMOTH

Jeremiah Barron grunted inaudibly and scanned the proceedings. The special session of the Plimoth Court was almost in session, and he took stock of the room. The audience of assembled townsfolk was larger than usual, and he was silently greeted by numerous unfamiliar faces. He diverted his bulbous eyes and cast his vision upon the wall and the great seal of Plimoth.

The great seal was created nine years after the arrival of the elect upon the colony's blessed shores. The most prominent feature of the design was Saint George's cross, and the depiction within of four Indians. Each was on one knee and holding a burning heart aloft. The burning heart was, of course, an homage to John Calvin and his famous seal. It signified the willingness to sacrifice in the service of the Almighty and was accentuated by the words "promptly and sincerely in the work of God." Barron had no doubt the court would function promptly and sincerely today.

He was a portly man of small to medium height and aged forty-two years. His family were seafaring merchants and traders, and he was one of the most prosperous men in the colony. Although blessed with material wealth, he was certainly not blessed in physical appearance. He bore a passing resemblance to Lord Protector Oliver Cromwell, but with an even more formidable nose and blemished, pock-marked skin. His hair was also unfortunate, a veritable mess of thin dark blonde strands manipulated to and fro in an inexplicable pattern. Finally, his unique voice was renowned throughout the colony for its high-pitched cacophony, leading the most gossipy of the Plimoth wives, in moments of lapsed Christian decorum, to refer to him as the "screech owl."

If the screech owl was aware of the opprobrious title bestowed upon him by the womenfolk, he made no inkling of it. He led his life as directed by the heavens above, a ceaseless rigor of what he liked to call the "five P's of his life": Piety, productivity, prayer, Plimoth and profit. Mrs. Barron was certainly disappointed every time he recited his mantra that there didn't seem to be any room for pleasure or passion.

Rigor and order were key attributes of the Plimoth General Court. Every year in March, the governor and seven assistants were elected. Subsequently, they appointed a number of lesser officials, such as messengers and constables. Although the duties of constables were quite apparent, the duties of the messengers were remarkably diverse. They might conduct land surveys, act as jailers (with all the authority to execute the appropriate punishments), and they might also disseminate announcements pertaining to the public interest such as marriage engagements and fatalities. Of course, one of the seven assistants was annually appointed to the role of treasurer of the colony, and Barron, perhaps through divine intervention, had served as treasurer for six consecutive years.

Barron focused his attention on the governor and awaited the call to order. Governor Thomas Prence was an astounding seventy years old. He had migrated to the New World a year after the Mayflower, and he naturally exuded a remarkable aura of history, dignity, and authority. His legacy as governor was well established. With regard to accusations and trials for witchcraft, his reputation was one of fairness and justice. During the Quaker crisis of recent decades, he performed admirably in ensuring their pernicious influence was adequately repressed. Under his guidance, the General Court enacted a death penalty for exiled Quakers who returned, but much to Barron's disappointment, it was never enforced.

Prence's policies regarding the savages, however,

proved to be a constant disappointment to Barron. Missionaries to the Indians described the governor as "kind" and "gentle" in his polices. Even more disillusioning, Governor Prence presided over a seven-year moratorium on the sale of Indian lands to the colonists, a policy Barron and his allies found to be unproductive and misguided. And Barron certainly did have allies, and he cast a knowing glance at the assistant governor.

Assistant Governor Josiah Winslow cast a splendid figure. His dark blue doublet was magnificently accentuated with snow-white cuffs and a ruff collar. His intense brown eyes returned Barron's glance and acknowledged their like minds. Winslow was a tremendous presence in the room and a tremendous presence in the government. At age forty-three Winslow was only one year older than Barron but unlike the treasurer, Winslow appeared to be the picture of health and vitality. As a previous commander of Plimoth's military forces, and as a commissioner to the United Colonies of New England (the military alliance to repel and deter the heathens), he was assumed to be a certain successor to the geriatric Prence.

With minimal fanfare, Governor Prence called the special session to order. The first ten minutes were dedicated to devout prayer, and then more worldly business could be addressed. Barron ensured his mannerisms and bearing conveyed his piety and loyalty, but inside he could scarcely contain his contempt. He reassured himself with the knowledge that Prence would soon be shuffling off of this mortal coil, and soon the colony would once again have the required leadership and vision to reach its divine destiny. Barron surreptitiously complimented himself for his Shakespearean eloquence.

Governor Prence was soon conveying the grim news to the General Court. The security apparatus of the colony had been made aware, on good authority, that the savages, particularly Philip of the Wampanoag, were conspiring with one another and agitating for open warfare. Winslow seemed to sit upright and beam at the mention of "good authority." The colony was indeed blessed with a network of informants and sympathizers amidst the heathen. As if playing a part in a Stratford-on-Avon theatrical event, Barron rose to speak.

"Governor Prence, blessings upon you and this holy instrument of the people. I shan't speak out of turn, but these are indeed grave and troublesome rumors and I implore the court for additional detail."

Winslow promptly took his cue and stood to address the court. The colony was in possession of disturbing revelations and talk of war from Metacomet, henceforth referred to derisively as "King Philip." The deluded and half-mad King Philip was still persisting in his demented conspiracy that the colony had a role in his brother's sudden, fatal, and tragic sickness. He was taking stock of his munitions and sending agents across the land to meet and conspire with all manner of heathen, including the Nipmuc from the wilderness west of Boston, the Podunk of Connecticut, the Nashaway, and even the Wampanoag historical nemesis, the Narragansett of Rhode Island. Barron cleared his throat and was soon screeching.

"What madness is this? Governor, this in intolerable. Five decades! Half a century! For half a century we have been striving to bring civilization and the light of Christ to these heathen. We have taught them the way of the musket, and we have intervened in their incessant wars. We have sent missionaries, and we've taught them Christian modesty and decency, and how is our generosity answered? With threats of terror and savagery, which I fear is all the heathen will ever understand." Barron had the rapt attention of the room.

"Governor, your experience and wisdom is instrumental in these difficult times. The courage and strength of our fathers and grandfathers should serve as a model. Sir, certainly you recall the decisive action of Plimoth Colony the year you first arrived on these sacred shores?" Governor Prence nodded vacantly, unsure if he was expected to speak. Barron didn't give him the opportunity, and turned to face the chamber.

"In 1621, a mere year after our forefathers arrived on these shores, the Narragansett heathen decided to test the mettle of God's chosen people. I hope each and every one of you knows the tale. They sent us a snakeskin full of arrowheads, assuming that a young, fragile colony would be so fearful of warfare that we would cower in terror and acquiesce to their demands. And how did our elders respond? Did they send a party to negotiate? Did they send missionaries?" Barron had the room agitated to such a fever that a constable standing in the chamber spontaneously exclaimed "musket balls!" Barron was delighted.

"Indeed, my friend! Musket balls indeed. The heathen received the reply of the righteous, a parcel of musket balls. They received the message clearly and undoubtedly, and warfare was averted. Shall the chosen people of the Almighty be intimidated by this new treachery? Shall we teach this "King Philip" the lesson the Pequot wish they had learned sooner?" The chamber erupted in a very atypical display of cheers and exuberance.

All eyes turned to Governor Prence, but it was Winslow who rose to speak. "The situation is indeed loathsome. I remember like it was yesterday, but perhaps it was ten years ago that the great Massasoit stood before this court and beamed with pride as we bestowed rightful Christian names upon his sons. I remember the intense grief I personally felt as Massasoit perished and his young son Alexander, scarcely a year later, fell so suddenly ill. But now? Now I fear friend has become foe and our livelihood is in grave peril." Winslow paused for dramatic effect.

"Governor Prence, I believe our course is clear. It is

imperative we summon this "King Philip" to appear before this esteemed assembly to answer for this treachery. Additionally, since we have little historical precedent to accept the testimony of an unrepentant pagan, I move, nay, I demand we take measures to strip the Wampanoag of their firearms, and compel them to take sacred oaths, attesting to the authority of this colony and to the King of England. There can be no other way."

The room was abuzz with muted excitement. The assembly expected the Governor to sanction the rousing call to action from Winslow. Instead, the moment was interrupted by a quiet voice from the back of the room. "Governor, if I may rise." All heads turned and the room became silent.

The stranger appeared to be weary and cautious. He had entered the courtroom with an enormous sack of goods, and his haggard, unkempt appearance was the result of days of exhausting travel. Most arrived at the rational conclusion he was a peddler. He rose to speak.

"This is my first appearance before this illustrious body, and I am thankful for the opportunity to address it. Although my experience in matters of government is terribly limited, I am fearful our warlike overtures are counter-productive and displeasing in the eyes of the Lord."

Barron sighed profusely and rolled his bulbous eyes. "And what, stranger, pray-tell, is your name and station in this colony?"

Brewster felt keen embarrassment as he had forgotten to introduce himself before speaking. "Forgive me. Governor, ladies, gentlemen, esteemed members of the court. I am Israel Brewster of Middleborough. I..."

Barron was quick to interrupt. "And you are a peddler of some manner? Certainly, you know it is inappropriate to hawk your baubles here." Once again, Brewster was embarrassed, this time by the weighty sack of tools, fabric and nails for the congregation of Middleborough.

"No sir, I am the Reverend Israel Brewster of Middleborough. Forgive my appearance and my goods. I have been traveling far. I have been…" Brewster contemplated the merits of revealing his new association with the Reverend Mather. On one hand, it might instill him with a newfound aura of authority and wisdom. Conversely, the Plimoth authorities might resent any mention of their smug, haughty neighbors to the north. He wisely deferred. "I have been travelling." Winslow seemed vaguely unsettled, and was certain he knew this young Brewster from somewhere but was unable to make the connection.

"Although I am not wise in the ways of government and military matters, I must protest our manner and words. Blessed be the peacemakers, gentlemen. I have had ample opportunity to teach and minister to the natives from my station in Middleborough, and I sincerely doubt warfare holds any appeal to them. At times, they bear the perplexed innocence of a child, and at other times they lash out at their authorities in a child-like manner. But they have suffered gravely and only seek justice." Brewster took a deep breath and continued.

"They wish to know their ways and traditions will not be brazenly trampled underfoot. They seek truth and fairness in their land transactions, and they seek validation that their land is their property to manage as they see fit. Metacomet and the Wampanoag are weak with sickness, and their numbers, as you all know, are depleted. With every passing year, more are baptized and civilized, God be praised. To impulsively demand some new oath of loyalty, and to treat them like unfit children who are not to be trusted with firearms would be the gravest of insults. Governor, I implore you to pursue patience, temperance, and Christian love."

Brewster's diatribe certainly did not generate the fevered enthusiasm of Winslow's exhortation. The room fell silent and Barron, once again, took the lead.

"Brewster...Brewster...of Middleborough? Yes, yes I am familiar with your situation." Barron genuinely was familiar with Israel Brewster, as he made a point to accrue as much knowledge and information about his neighbors as humanly possible. "Reverend Brewster, thank you for addressing this court. Although I am certain your words are heartfelt, if you had the roles and responsibilities of ensuring the safety of this colony, I am sure you would come to realize how naïve and childish your worldview is.

"We bear you no ill will, for we know of your recent tragedy and grief. I would personally counsel that, perhaps it would be wise that, instead of focusing on stately matters of which you know nothing, perhaps your time would be better focused on your own life and salvation. Have your life and actions genuinely been pleasing to the Lord, Reverend? As the illustrious Reverend Mather counsels, the will and judgement of God is made manifest in every aspect of our lives. If we stray into wickedness and disobedience, the discipline of the Lord is steadfast and sure. Perhaps, you have come to terms with whatever disobedience so dramatically impacted you and your beloved?"

Brewster stood silently and was incapable of a response. He was aware of the mist in his eyes and his cheeks felt flush. How foolish had he been, this country bumpkin of a pastor, to try and address this holy and righteous assembly. Without a word, he resumed his seat and the deliberations continued. He was especially perplexed by the reference to Mather, as he was certain he did not mention their meeting. Was Jeremiah Barron aware of it already, or was the reference a mere coincidence?

Winslow asked if any other freemen wished to address the court. Unsurprisingly, none did. Also, unsurprisingly, Governor Prence concurred with Winslow's plans and the way ahead was finalized. King Philip would be summoned before this body and made to answer for his hostility. The special session concluded with a brief prayer, imploring the Almighty for strength in the face of the heathen. The meeting was adjourned and the assembly began to quietly disband. Brewster left the room without a word from anyone.

Barron carefully watched Brewster make his exit. He had grave concerns about this troublesome young man, and dissenters that threatened the livelihood of their society were not to be taken lightly.

His machinations were interrupted by Winslow. "Jeremiah, our guest is here and wishes a word. Shall we repair to your workplace?"

Within minutes Jeremiah Barron and Assistant Governor Winslow were seated in the office of the Treasurer of Plimoth Colony, and enjoying a fine glass of port. Standing before them was the elegant and refined Elijah MacTavish, who owned and directed the largest collection of sugar plantations in Bermuda. After some introductory small talk during which MacTavish complained incessantly, belittling the Plimoth weather, food and architecture, it was time for business.

"Friends, I know you have your curiosity regarding the sugar trade in Bermuda. You wish to know the status of your investments and rightfully so. Be assured, the profitability is staggering and Europe's appetite for sweetness was severely underestimated. I am confident your investments will quadruple in value before the next planting." His hosts nodded their pleasure.

"Ahh, but manpower. As with any undertaking these days, labor is at a premium. Countless opportunities beckon for more planting, more sugar cane and more profit, but labor is a ceaseless drain. I'm afraid the demand for Africans on these shores as well as the Caribbean has become so great that the cost of the resource is impacting profitability. You can imagine the dilemma of the gentlemen planters.

"The Indians of New England, however, have been

serving our interests very well. Some believe the Pequot shipped to us two decades ago are suited only to the role of household servants, but I am confident with the right training and motivation, the natives of New England can generate as much productive labor in the fields as their counterparts from across the sea.

"I know you wish no unholy malice upon your neighbors, and you are fair in your dealings. I only wish to reinforce the truth that, should the opportunity of supply arise, I dare say the market is there. I implore you consider, that, should another conflict arise in the manner of the Pequots, what of the vanquished? Certainly, the will of God dictates victory for Plimoth and the United Colonies. What is to become of hundreds, if not thousands of defeated, treasonous savages? They will always be a hideous impediment to civilization's progress and a vile, loathsome threat to your welfare.

"But I have blathered for far too long. Gentlemen! A toast!" He raised his port in the air, then lowered it just as quickly. "Forgive me, this New England climate is impacting my faculties. I have forgotten to mention a preliminary return on your investments. Although the first monetary disbursement will not be sanctioned until next year, I have procured some valuable property as a token of good faith."

Unbeknownst to Winslow and Barron, on the dockside of Plimoth, were two timid African girls of approximately fifteen years of age. They were awaiting transport to their new homes and their new lives as English household servants for two of the finest families in Plimoth. MacTavish raised his glass again.

"To the prosperity of Plimoth Colony!"

CHAPTER SEVEN

MONTAUP

Metacomet strode deliberately and hurriedly into the woods. He did not turn to scan the activity behind him, for he fully expected Linto would be trailing him as commanded. The Sachem was correct, and Linto anxiously sped up to catch him.

After several moments of walking in silence, the distance grew between the two men and the dispersing council. Tobias stared vacantly after them, while Mentayyup went in search of more roasted trout. Linto could not find the fortitude to speak, and he wondered how long his Sachem would remain silent. The meeting of the council had been fascinating for Linto, for though he had known since childhood Wamsutta had perished at the hands of the English, he had never heard the events recounted in such detail. He felt tremendous sympathy for the burden Mentayyup had carried these long years, though faultless in every aspect. Finally, when Linto thought he could bear no more, Metacomet stopped in a clearing under three massive maple trees.

"You are a turtle, Linto."

Linto smiled and protested. "You stormed off without me, but I caught you soon enough." Before his sentence was even finished he realized his foolishness. "Oh. The clan." Linto was adopted into both the Wampanoag people, and the turtle clan.

"These visions, Linto. They require guidance. Spiritual guidance, for I am as confused as ever. I am tired of feeling directionless and tormented in front of my people."

"Sachem, there are so many powwas in the clan. What do I know of these things?" He was greeted by sullen silence and the walking resumed. Linto kept an eye on the skies as he was certain rain was imminent. A cool breeze was gaining strength from the north. Finally, after walking at least two hundred paces, Linto could take no more. He stopped and looked Metacomet in the eye.

"Where were you, Sachem?"

The question required no clarification and Metacomet sighed. "After Weetamoo received the news, she sent a runner to Titicut. Although swift, news was quite delayed because Titicut was not our original plan. We had planned to camp to the west by Sabbatia Lake. The hunting was poor, however, and after two nights we migrated to Titicut. After we received word, we moved like the wind toward Plimoth. We had, however, missed Weetamoo and Wamsutta. We turned to the west to rendezvous, but..." He had no need to finish the sentence.

"What does it mean, Linto? Why is he soaring and I am falling? Why would he taunt me in my dreams?" Linto was speechless and gazed upward, hoping for cool rain to break the awkwardness.

"Linto, when will you embrace your destiny? Yes, there are powwas throughout the Wampanoag. They are older than you, they have endured more than you, and they claim to be wiser than you. They tell me how unreceptive you have been to their instruction, and how you will never serve our people as a powwas." Linto could not deny it. He spent his days questioning rather than learning, demanding instead of accepting. When he should have been studying medicinal herbs and prophecy, he was hunting or rebuilding wetus.

Metacomet continued. "The time is now, Linto. I am in need of divine guidance, now more than ever. I have told you for years what you have meant to me and our people. Embrace your destiny, Linto."

Twenty summers ago, Metacomet was completing the rites of manhood in the tribe. His physical prowess was formidable for one his age, and even though he was a mere thirteen summers in age, there was little he did not know about hunting and fishing. He was truly, like Wamsutta, the son of a Sachem, and Massasoit was enormously proud.

During a brutally hot and dry summer, Massasoit led a party of twenty Wampanoag north. The mission was varied. They would trade with their neighbors, as always. They would make diplomatic overtures to the nations to help ensure the peace, especially among those jealous and suspicious of their alliance with Plimoth. And they would monitor and explore the shifting balances of power, as the vile European diseases had been plaguing the land for more than thirty summers. Tribal nations often sent delegations to one another to survey the impact of the plagues, to offer assistance and kinship, and to (somewhat desperately) ascertain what healing discoveries were to be found, if any.

As such, Massasoit was accompanied by no fewer than seven prominent members of the turtle and bear clans. They brought medicinal tonics and they brought spiritual wisdom, but the sad reality was that despite their divine supplications to the heavens, they had no answers and the Wampanoag were suffering horrifically. The English called it smallpox, and it was pure death to the nations.

Even before the English landed and built their homesteads at Patuxet, Massasoit's people were dying. The Sachem could not stand to contemplate the death toll. Four out of ten? Six out of ten? Feelings of misery and confusion alternated with anger, shame, and abandonment. What had they done for such horror to befall them? Had they not lived in the balance and harmony the Great Spirit demanded? Was this the divine will of the English God and his gentle Son? Perhaps the land was meant for the English after all.

At the right hand of Massasoit during the expedition was Metacomet. It was evident that Metacomet would soon be taller than his father, and Massasoit was overjoyed. They were heading north, very far north, to visit the Abenaki nation, to the Penacook people and the village of Ossinak, which was a day's journey from Squawkeag. The journey had taken an entire moon, and they had spent many days feasting and trading with the Nipmuc prior to resuming their northerly trek.

The Abenaki nation spanned a tremendous swath of land and Massasoit's company would be visiting the southern tip of the western Abenaki. The village was near the banks of the mighty north-south river the English had named the Connecticut. The Abenaki were known as the "people of the dawn land," as their nation extended east to the sea. The Wampanoag had reason to believe the western Abenaki were especially ravaged by the English plagues but contact had been minimal over the previous years, and they were anxious to reaffirm good tidings and hopefully share in their renowned talent for salmon fishing.

The company was approximately four hundred paces from Ossinak, when Wantuk, the most elder powwas, shuddered and collapsed to the ground. She was quickly revived, and she claimed she could feel a sense of horrific suffering. Undeterred, the company proceeded onward and was greeted by the unmistakable aura of death.

Corpses were everywhere throughout the village of Ossinak, and the death came so totally and rapidly that bodies were left where they fell. Those who had died within a few days bore the unmistakable visage of smallpox. Others were decomposed beyond recognition. Metacomet, the tall, brave son of the Sachem, promptly fell to his knees and vomited. Amidst the death were remarkable signs of lives interrupted. Salmon left untouched. Deerskin leggings half completed. Homes started but left in a chaotic state. The Wampanoag peered in dwellings and behind trees. They called out, but there was not a human soul to be found.

Gathering his faculties, young Metacomet rose to his feet and could see the tears welling in his father's dark eyes. Perhaps as sickening as the smell, as sickening as the sights, was the silence. The eerie, unrelenting silence. And then there was singing.

The voice was so unexpected and so bizarre the company gaped at one another, silently clamoring for an explanation. This was not a death anthem of a village elder, or a sad entreaty to the Great Spirit bellowed by a wizened powwas. This was the joyful merriment of a small child. Although there was a language barrier, the Wampanoag were certain it was, as the English would call it, a "nursery rhyme"- a simple, happy little ditty meant to impart *giggles to small children.*

The singing seemed to be getting louder and Metacomet cautiously trailed his father as he and Wantuk peered into the shadowy, unexplored corner of the home. Was it a phantom? Metacomet tried to keep his distance, but his curiosity overwhelmed him. His fears quickly disintegrated, for there in the corner, partially covered in a ragged blanket was a child of about two or three summers. His hair was long and chaotic and his face was filthy. But completely oblivious to his surroundings, as if in a world of his own, he sang. If the Wampanoag could understand his language, they would have heard:

"Sing Sing Sing! Sing a song for the birds"
"Sing Sing Sing! And they will sing right back."

Instead, with the language barrier, all they heard and retained was, "Linto Linto Linto!" Wantuk picked the child from the ground and it squealed with delight, and she declared the boy to be a miracle, a divinely sanctioned, holy being meant to convey hope in an age of catastrophe and death. Massasoit took him in his arms, held him aloft, and sang out "Linto, Linto, Linto! What a man you shall be." And Metacomet knew then and there that their spirits and ancestors had not abandoned them, and there would be hope for their future.

Linto sullenly stared at the ground. He had heard it all before. How many times and ways had he heard the story? He was special. He was adopted. He was a miracle, placed in the care of the Wampanoag for reasons to be revealed one day. And he hated every word.

He did not feel special. Linto did not feel gifted, divine, miraculous, or wise. He would never know why this fate was foisted upon him. Linto just wanted to hunt, fish, and eat all day, and at night all he wanted was to dance and lay under his fur cloak with Wawetseka. He had no prophecy to offer. He had no holy insights to give. Metacomet could see his discomfort, and he diverted the topic.

"I have sent delegations across the lands. Did you

know that, Linto?" Linto was uncertain what to say. He, like all with their ears intact, heard rumblings of alliances and rebellion. "We have negotiated with the Nipmuc, the Podunk…even with the Narragansett and…" Metacomet left his sentence unfinished.

"The Abenaki?"

"Yes, Linto. The Abenaki. And I have personally met with Wamsutta's widow. Her rage still boils but her husband, Petonowit, has sympathies with the English. I will never understand how they stay together under one roof."

"Don't we have sympathies with the English, Sachem?" It was such a simple question but Metacomet felt like he had been clubbed.

"I don't know, Linto. Perhaps we are the hypocrites? Perhaps we want the English muskets, and fine clothes, and tools, and cooking pots, and knives, and books. We want the rum. We want all the good things that come with selling off our land, but when the land is gone, what then?

"My visions torment me, Linto. Tobias and Mentayyup would slice English throats tonight if I gave the word. But Sassamon is so learned and speaks such wisdom. I cannot betray the alliance of my father, but I cannot bear any more English fraud and contempt. And the situation will get worse, for I know the English have their spies everywhere, and with every whisper of rebellion they load their muskets. They would love a war. Their big, ancient book tells them to love their neighbors, and it tells them to slaughter the enemies of their God. No wonder they are so two-faced." Linto nodded earnestly.

"Are you going to attend their Christian talk, Linto?" Linto nodded again. The Sachem was referring to the imminent missionary trip in Cohannet, which the English called Taunton.

"I enjoy those things. I like learning English, and the food is good. Everyone is nice, Sachem, especially the women." Metacomet did not resent Linto partaking in the Christian outreach. Linto was divinely blessed, and if he could ascertain the will of the English God, and could comprehend the divine plan of the plagues, so much the better. As the Sachem, however, Metacomet had a sacred duty to the religion of his forefathers.

Metacomet changed the subject. "Do you know what happened to my father two summers after the English arrived? Have you ever heard the tale, Linto?" Linto admitted he had not.

"Two summers after the English arrived in their mighty boat, my father Massasoit, the greatest of Sachems, was on his deathbed. There were even rumors he had perished. Do you know what happened next, Linto? Winslow the father came immediately. He scraped the disease from my father's mouth. He nourished him with magical English concoctions, and my father was well again. Perhaps I would not even be here speaking with you without Winslow the father. But when I think of Winslow the son..." Metacomet left the sentence unfinished.

"Linto, I am pleading with you. Think back to my dreams. What do they mean? Some tell me Wamsutta is mocking me because I'm like a child and afraid of the English. Some tell me if I lead the nations to war it would be like leaping off a cliff. Tell me, Linto. Please tell me. What should I do?"

The rain finally began to gently fall. Linto tried to fully appreciate the position he was in. His powers at that moment were awesome. He had no doubt if he told Metacomet that the time to avenge the filthy English for the murder of Wamsutta was upon them, then there would be a council of war that night. If he said Sassamon offered the wisest words, and the English were the best hope for their prosperity, then it would be so. He believed if he told his Sachem that the five prettiest girls of the Wampanoag should be delivered to Linto for divine, lustful rituals that only Linto could comprehend, the Sachem would comply without question. With all of this hanging over him, Linto opted for the only course he had the courage to pursue. He decided to tell the truth.

"I have no idea, Sachem. Forgive me, but I have no idea."

CHAPTER EIGHT

TAUNTON

Brewster was elated. Today was a day he had been fervently anticipating, perhaps even more so than his sojourn to Boston. Brewster would lead the congregation on a missionary trip to Taunton, ten miles west of Middleborough. The participation of the congregation seemed to exceed his hopes, as he would be leading two dozen of God's saints westward. Even the typically anemic carpenter, Reddington, found the spiritual energy to make the journey. Brewster was also delighted to receive word the most elite missionary in the colony, Reverend John Eliot, would be attending, and even the Plimoth General Court was sending a representative, the learned Reverend Peter Phelps. And of course, the lovely Alice Fuller would be riding by Brewster's side.

In addition to the tools, fabric, and nails Brewster procured from Boston, he surreptitiously acquired a Scottish plaid broach. It was a thing of rare beauty. Brewster was uncertain why the merchant described it as "plaid," as there was certainly no evidence of such a pattern. It was perfectly round and symmetrical in every respect. It was accentuated with silver and amethyst, with interlocking patterns Brewster could scarcely fathom. It cost him the equivalent of a week's wages, but he had to have it.

Alice was delighted with the gift and said it was the most beautiful thing she had ever owned, and perhaps the most beautiful thing she had ever seen. As the gift was from a devout clergyman, she quickly revised her assessment to exclude all of the majestic beauty the Lord had created. Brewster, though tormented by night terrors even more persistently than usual, had increasingly considered the public courtship of this beauty.

He exuded an aura of confidence as he rode atop Brownie on this breezy day. He had become quite acclimated to his time with Brownie and could increasingly anticipate her every quirk and anxiety. Brewster still brooded over the unfortunate name. He stared at her mane and contemplated the array of names better suited to her. His mind turned to Shakespeare, and there was soon a mental torrent of delightful, exquisite names. *Cressida. Ophelia. Rosalind, Portia and Bianca.* Yet here he was with…Brownie.

Brewster's spirit had recovered quite promptly from the public rebuke in Plimoth. He had no doubt many in Middleborough were tittering about it, but so be it. He had spoken his conscience as the Lord bade him, and many in his township could empathize, as they too often felt the unmistakable sting of their government's righteousness. Brewster had been disciplined, and he resolved to remain silent in the face of colonial security matters.

After departing shortly after dawn, the mission party arrived approximately three hours later. There were songs and good-spirited camaraderie enroute, and Brewster could not be happier. He made it a point to mingle throughout, and not devote himself exclusively to Alice. Her father had brought at least twenty pounds of various smoked meats, and their native friends would relish the bounty.

The mission trip was organized on the eastern shore of Richmond Pond, and the location paid dividends. The scenic beauty was spectacular, and there was ample open space for trading, foot races, archery, wrestling, and feasting. There seemed to be approximately four dozen natives in attendance. Brewster believed they were almost exclusively Wampanoag, but he lacked the expertise for proper discernment.

Reverend Eliot had, as expected, beaten them handily to the site. John Eliot was blessed, or cursed, with an appearance that usually brought smiles to a stranger's face. For a devout missionary, he was remarkably rotund, a condition he ascribed to the "incessant gratitude and generosity of the saved wretches of the colony." His face was framed by stringy strands of mostly gray hair, parted carelessly through the middle of his head. Strangers who met him often debated whether he had a moustache, was in the process of growing a moustache, or merely had his upper lip stained by some recent morsel. His round eyes seemed to routinely alternate between joy, somber worship, and prankish mischief. Though he had spent more than six decades on this earth, approximately four of which were spent in the new world, he still boasted tireless energy.

Shortly after arriving in the new world, Reverend Eliot focused some of his tireless energy on the issue of Antinomianism, which the residents of the colony recalled as the "free grace" unorthodoxy. Reverend Eliot was passionate and eloquent on the topic, and Brewster knew the result was the exile of the free-thinking Anne Hutchinson. In these later days, however, Eliot seemed to focus on the salvation of the natives, and he was a tremendous advocate for the Christianized "praying Indians" and the consolidation of the Christianized natives in "praying towns." His language skills were remarkable, and he brought at least twenty copies of his famous bible translation. He was discussing the sermon on the mount, reading loudly from the book of Matthew.

After a hug and blessing from Eliot, Brewster jumped right into the fray. He led his Middleborough team in psalmody, and the natives seemed politely fascinated. Brewster had been fervently studying the local dialect, and he successfully taught four young women the first verse of the Lord's Prayer in their native tongue.

> "N∞shun kesukqut
> Wunneetupantamunach k∞wesuonk
> Peyaum∞utch kukkeitass∞tam∞onk.
> Toh anantaman ne naj okheit, neane kesukqut"

He ate the delicacies the Wampanoag brought, and with the assistance of Eliot, he recounted the testimony of the empty tomb and resurrection. He frequently caught Alice's eye, and felt he might burst with joy. He even remembered to procure some Summer Savory herb for the Farwells, to assist with their matrimonial issues.

The saints of God were mindful to mix their ministry with a healthy dose of carefree activity in order to support their objective: An open-minded, attentive audience soon to embrace Christian repentance and discipleship. Brewster smiled as the foot races raged in every direction, and was stunned when a burly Wampanoag of approximately his age dragged him into a wrestling bout.

Brewster was inclined to formulate an excuse to recuse himself, but he feared any lapse in decorum might negatively impact the success of the missionary activities, so he quickly acquiesced. His opponent motioned for Brewster to remove his shirt, and Brewster mentally fought the notion before casting his Puritan modesty to the wind. His opponent laughed and jeered as he tossed Brewster about like a rag doll, despite Brewster's best efforts, and his fervent hope of impressing Alice. Soon the victor was bored, and gave way to a second kinsman, who seemed to be about seventeen years old and stood a foot shorter than Brewster.

Brewster was horrified to discover the result was just the same, as the youngster exhibited a speed and wiry strength that left Brewster breathless and defeated again. Once again, Brewster's opponent seemed bored of the challenge and gave way to a handsome man of about twenty years.

He was slender and tall, and he cast a hypnotic smile at Brewster as Brewster stood hunched with his hands on his knees, gasping for breath. This opponent seemed familiar to Brewster, and he was almost certain they had met during a previous missionary service. He seemed content to wait for the twice-defeated Englishman to compose himself, and soon the match was on.

Brewster knew very little about this Wampanoag style of wrestling, but he did know he was tired of winding up on the ground. His mind wandered to the Biblical warriors of great renown, and he was determined to generate a Samsonesque burst of strength that would vanquish this adversary and remove the incessant smile from his face. Brewster feinted a left shoulder throw, but just as quickly fell to the ground and twisted his opponent's powerful leg until his balance was lost and he collapsed to the ground. Brewster held him to the cool earth, and then stood triumphantly in a mighty demonstration of victory.

The vanquished wrestler seemed unable to stand, but remained on his back, staring at the sky and smiling more broadly than ever. Brewster was surprised when he called out in passable English, "Two Ponds! Help me up, Two Ponds!" The perplexed Englishman extended his arm and pulled him upright, and the grinning Wampanoag dusted himself clean. "Such a mighty display, Englishman." His eyes seemed to drift from Brewster to the engrossed Alice Fuller, and he paused to ensure his words had registered. "Two Ponds, I am Linto. It is an Abenaki name. I am anxious to hear more of your thoughts on the English God's gentle Son."

Brewster's confusion was not dissipating and he responded. "I fear you may have me confused with another Englishman. My name is Reverend Israel Brewster of Middleborough, and I know nothing of Two Ponds." Linto responded that as far as he was concerned, Brewster was now "Two Ponds", as Linto had met numerous white colonists, but he had never seen enormous blue eyes like Brewster's.

The Reverend Brewster saw no need to condemn or resist his new title, and he could only smile with Linto. Alice was soon whisked away by a legion of womenfolk anxious to serve another meal, while Linto and Brewster strode together to the edge of the pond. Brewster put his shirt back on, and they were soon joined by one of the loveliest creatures Brewster ever cast eyes upon, whom Linto introduced as Wawetseka. Her English was poor and she seemed to be at the periphery of the conversation. Linto, however, had spent hours of study with Sassamon and had quietly become one of the premier speakers of English among the Wampanoag.

"Two Ponds, I have attended so many missionary visits, and I fear I am growing less wise and more confused. Sassamon is always reading to me from the big book, and perhaps I am not smart enough to be a Christian like him." Brewster could not let that remark go unanswered.

"Then Jesus called a little child to Him, set him in the midst of them, and said, *Assuredly, I say to you, unless you are converted and become as little children, you will by no means enter the kingdom of heaven. Therefore, whoever humbles himself as this little child is the greatest in the kingdom of heaven.*"

"Two Ponds, the words are beautiful, but I do not understand how God the Father seems so angry and jealous, and God the Son seems so kind and forgiving. They remind me of Tobias and his son." Brewster wondered if this was a good moment for commentary, but he chose to let Linto continue. "We are told God the Father knows everything. He has planned everything. He knows who will die and who will go to heaven. Why are my people so sick? Was it his will that so many of us would get sick and die after we met the white men from across the sea?" Brewster mentally sought a Biblical passage that would allay Linto's concerns, but he was at a loss.

"Did the white men ever suffer such a plague across the sea? Were they ever made to suffer as we?" Brewster recounted the history of the Black Death, which left Europe helpless more than three centuries ago, and depleted a third of the population. Linto had never heard of it, and Brewster could not ascertain if the thought brought him comfort or more anxiety. Wawetseka was staring at Brewster as if she had never seen an Englishman before.

"Two Ponds, I am supposed to be a holy man among my people. It gnaws at me. I want to reject it. I'm not sure I understand the English God, or the Great Spirit, or Wendigo, or anything. Wawetseka is so much more gifted than I in matters of prophecy and healing. Sassamon told me about the elections of God. Why does God need to vote?"

"I'm sorry? Elections?"

"They say God believes mankind is wicked and sinful. I am not so sure about that. I like almost everyone I meet, even the English. Sometimes Tobias worries me, though, because he seems so angry. But Sassamon told me God has already had elections, and He knows who will be saved, and who will be punished forever?"

Brewster finally understood. "The elect. Indeed, mankind is wicked and sinful, and God, in His infinite mercy, has pre-ordained..."Brewster chose a less lofty word. "God has known since the beginning of time who was chosen to be saved and who will perish."

"Are you elected?"

Brewster sighed. "I believe I have lived a life pleasing to God in both word and deed. I have accepted my blessed assurance."

"But why should people do the things God demands if they might have not been elected anyway? Why did He create so many people if they weren't going to be elected? Why did He create smallpox?"

Brewster rubbed his blue eyes. This was not one of his better outreaches. "Linto, have you heard and accepted the word of God? Do you understand the love of Christ Jesus, born of a virgin and raised from the dead?"

"I have to admit I liked the hilltop talk quite a bit."

"The what?"

"Blessed are the poor in spirit. That's very nice."

"The sermon on the mount. Yes, it is very inspirational."

"I like it when the gentle Son talks about His father's kingdom. He said people are blessed when they are persecuted for being right, and the kingdom of heaven belongs to them. I also like the part about blessing those who have grief, because they will be comforted. We have known so much grief, Two Ponds."

Brewster wondered if the hauntingly beautiful young woman was understanding any of this. Her eyes did not leave his. Linto noticed the object of Brewster's attention.

"Two Ponds, are you married?" Brewster actually blushed and turned away. Before he could answer, Linto continued, "or do you prefer the company of men?" Brewster assumed the remark to be innocent, but he knew the natives to be much more tolerant of that abomination than God's chosen people. As such, it was a recurring topic during missionary visits.

"I had a wife, very recently, but she is...with the Lord." Linto nodded solemnly and Wawetseka began to gently cry.

"Wawetseka and I will be married soon. Metacomet has blessed our union."

Brewster was relieved to discuss a topic other than predestination. "And how is your esteemed Sachem? Healthy and well, I pray?"

"Frankly, Two Ponds, these are difficult days. The Sachem continues to be tormented by the death of his brother, Wamsutta. He dreams dreams, and he mutters aimlessly when he thinks he is alone. I think Wawetseka should heal him, but he has not permitted it. He says his grief is an inseparable part of him."

"Wamsutta? That was...nine or ten years ago? And he is still grieving?"

"His dreams haunt him. Deep down, he thinks Skunk Genitals killed him. We all do."

"Who?"

"Winslow. Winslow the son. He took Wamsutta away, and then Wamsutta died. It must have been poison."

"The Wampanoag believe Assistant Governor Winslow murdered their Sachem? For nine years, they've believed this?" Brewster turned away and looked out at the pond. He was suddenly troubled.

"Linto, there is something I have spoken about with very few people. Almost nobody."

"You love Alice with the dark eyes? Yes, we all know that. You stare at her like a little puppy."

Brewster seemed unamused by the levity. He was lost in his thoughts and began pacing. He stared out across the water and he distractedly ran his fingers though his dark hair.

Finally, he spoke. "No, Linto. Wamsutta. I was there with him, Linto. Wamsutta. Plimoth."

"You were what?"

"I was there. I was with Skunk...I was with Winslow. I think I was your age, even younger. I was doing my militia duty for the colony. I was so timid, I could barely even point a musket. We were patrolling the area west of Duxbury when Major Winslow...he's the assistant governor now...Major Winslow received reports that Wamsutta was at a hunting camp. Major Winslow was very eager to bring him to Plimoth for questioning, but his intent was not malicious. The government had been hearing very unsettling rumors.

"Things were very tense when we arrived and I was very nervous. Wamsutta was wonderful in the way he defused the crisis, and he voluntarily accompanied us. Major Winslow intended to present him with a sumptuous meal at his home, but Wamsutta became fatigued shortly after we left the hunting camp.

"I remember the doctor was called. I think he is actually a relation to Alice. The doctor gave him...what did he call it? Umm..."

"A potion of a working physic. For his humours."

"That's it! Yes! How did you know? Remarkable! Oh, how that potion smelled. After we left Duxbury, Wamsutta was on horseback enroute to Plimoth. I remember he took the sealed jar from his satchel. He opened it and grimaced like he would vomit. He noticed I was watching him, and he grinned at me. He laughed, then tried to gather his energy. He then threw the jar as far as he could into the woods. Major Winslow was twenty yards ahead and had no idea." Linto was looking at Brewster as if Brewster was floating above the ground.

"He threw it away?"

"Oh, goodness yes. I think we could still smell it ten minutes later. After we got to Plimoth Wamsutta seemed to be getting worse. He could barely stand in the court, and the magistrates soon grew weary of trying to interrogate him. They ordered him cared for in the nicest bed available, and they sent for another physician.

"I was with him almost every minute, from the time he left the hunting camp until the time the lady chief came for him. Oh my, what a terror she was. But Wamsutta was never able or willing to eat or drink anything. He wouldn't even take water. It was so terrible though, watching him fade away. I will never forget the anguish of his wife, the lady chief. I don't even know if he was able to speak after she took him away. I still remember the things he told me before he died, though. He could barely whisper, and he made me lean in. But I remember it to this day. I remember every word. I can't wrestle for beans, Linto, but I can tell you every name in the Holy Bible, that's the memory I've been blessed with. He said:

"*You have offered me much but I have accepted nothing. You have seen this with your own eyes. Though my destiny is closed, my fault is with the heavens. I have not been corrupted…no…mackiki… by the English. Ensure the people understand and bear no ill tidings.*"

Brewster continued. "I thought it was beautiful, but mysterious. Such a statement of pride. I have not been corrupted by the English. No mockery. His faculties were fading quickly, though. He couldn't recall how to say *mockery*." Linto grabbed Brewster by the shoulders and shook him furiously.

"And who did you tell? Did you tell anyone these words?"

Brewster was stunned, but he retained his composure. "I recounted them verbatim to my militia captain. I asked if we should tell Major Winslow, but the captain said it sounded like…" Brewster lowered his voice to a whisper. *"It sounded like the bitter complaints of another dead Indian, and Major Winslow shouldn't be bothered with such nonsense.* He was the only one I ever told. Him and…Sarah. Sarah, my wife."

Linto was clearly agitated, and he implored Brewster to repeat the words in their entirety two more times. "Mockery! Mockery! Don't you get it, Two Ponds? He wasn't saying *mockery,* he couldn't remember the English word for poison! He said the Wampanoag word for poison! Mackiki! He knew how suspicious we would be, because his health failed so quickly! Listen to his words. *I have accepted nothing…my destiny is closed…ensure the people understand!* Can't you see it Two Ponds? Finally! I finally have something to tell my Sachem! Wamsutta was not poisoned!"

Brewster was finally comprehending. "And he will believe my testimony?"

"He will believe me, for I am a holy man." Linto threw his head back and laughed, but his momentary joy was interrupted, for Wawetseka looked more anguished than ever. Her eyes were still moist and she whispered to Linto in words Brewster could not understand. He looked concerned, and eyeing Brewster, nodded vigorously.

"Two Ponds, my partner Wawetseka can feel the pain radiating from your soul. It is causing her anguish. She can see the nightmares and begs that she may be permitted to heal you." Brewster was too stunned to speak.

"She understands the cause of your torment, and she has implored you undergo the sacred ceremony of healing. She is very skilled, Two Ponds. She has a gift."

"I...really must be getting back. There is still much to do."

"Two Ponds, I beg you. Please stop your arrogance. You English are afraid of whatever you don't understand. You come and tell us about strong men who had their hair cut and then weren't strong anymore. You tell us about boats filled with animals and floods, and men who live in the belly of a whale. You think we are ignorant children, and yet your grandfather would have starved to death in Patuxet if we did not pity and intervene.

"Two Ponds, you are suffering and your pain is real. You must undergo this ritual. Do not deny this. I am leaving you in her custody, and I am going to find a boat to go see Metacomet. I must run as fast as my legs can carry me."

Without another word Wawetseka took Brewster by the hand. Linto hugged him farewell and thanked him profusely. And Brewster whispered his farewell.

"Linto, the next time you let me win a wrestling match, make it look better. I don't think Alice bought it for a minute."

CHAPTER NINE

TAUNTON

Brewster felt strangely alone after Linto took his leave. He watched him flee the scene, and was certain he had never seen another human being run so fast. Within a matter of seconds Linto was out of sight, and Wawetseka had tightened her grip on his hand which had begun to slightly quiver.

She was leading him east of Richmond Pond away from the water, away from the activity, and away from his congregation. Brewster could still hear the echoes of Reverend Eliot, his baritone resonating throughout the gathering. He could view Alice Fuller, who was sharing a plate of glazed apples with Reverend Phelps. She stood as she made eye contact, and Reverend Phelps turned to see the object of her attention. Her expression simultaneously conveyed befuddlement, consternation, and a noteworthy portion of wrath.

Wawetseka wordlessly motioned across the field to an elderly Wampanoag woman. She nodded her comprehension and seemed to be gathering supplies. Brewster thought intently about forcing this quiet young woman to release her grip, but Linto's tirade had somehow rendered him meek and compliant. They were soon embraced by the cool shadows of the forest. Brewster felt the overwhelming urge to say something to break the silence, and he inquired how long she would require him. His question went unanswered, and he was left wondering if she could comprehend English. He felt foolish and returned to speechlessly admiring her beauty and grace.

Within minutes they were deep in the forest, and Brewster was startled to see the elderly Wampanoag woman had found them. He did not know much detail about the tribal roles, but he assumed she was a powwas of some kind and held authority over Wawetseka. She knelt to build a small fire, and Brewster was awestruck by the speed and skill she applied to the task. Soon the heat radiated, and the light cast unsettling shadows around the trio. The powwas was now brewing a tea of some kind, and Brewster could not recognize the herbs.

Wawetseka had finally released his hand, and she gently forced him to kneel on the soft ground. Brewster had strong reservations about his cooperation in this ritual and thought long and hard about sprinting to safety. Wawetseka was in the process of removing his shirt, and his mind reeled as he imagined the promiscuity that may very well plague her people. She was now gently caressing his temples and neck, and Brewster felt deep shame as the pleasurable sensations radiated through him. An unwanted stirring emerged in his loins. With the exception of Alice Fuller's slender, delicate hand, he had not felt the touch of a woman in eighteen months. He tried desperately to focus and formulate a way to extricate himself from this unholy circumstance in the most Christian manner possible.

The tea was now complete, and it was obvious to Brewster that only one serving had been prepared. Clearly at this moment, his faculties and reasoning were still intact. It was not too late to end this madness. This was the moment in which he would nod politely, stand up, don his shirt, and march proudly back to the missionary services. He would minister to these pagans and provide holy guidance, but he certainly would not partake in their sinful customs.

He then took the tea and drank it all in one gulp.

Wawetseka was guiding his head to the forest floor, where she had fashioned a serviceable pillow from his shirt and pine straw. He stared straight up, through the tall, beautiful monuments of the Lord's handiwork. He cursed his actions, his impulsivity, and the trust he placed in these mysterious strangers. He relentlessly and naively clung to a fading hope that the tea was merely a nutrient, and every bit as innocent as the cup he shared with Reverend Mather last week.

Wawetseka was caressing his temples again and chanting, and Brewster somehow derived comfort from the revelation she knew at least some English. "Heal thy spirit…heal thyself. Shhh…Heal thy spirit…heal thyself." Her elder was chanting as well, and Brewster could not comprehend her words. She stirred the fire and the flames grew higher. Brewster could no longer deny the trees were spinning, and he could no longer hear the women. He moaned and closed his eyes.

It was so cold. Bitter, frigid, astounding cold. Even in New England, this final week of November had been unusually cruel.

Brewster resolved to pay it no mind and the pace of his wood-splitting quickened. As usual, his thoughts wandered to Grandfather Brewster and the first winter at Plimoth. Israel Brewster had never set foot in England or Europe, but he knew they were no stranger to the wrath of the season. Yet he could not imagine their time in England or Holland could have prepared them for this wilderness. The merciless cold and snow of this new world must have been incomprehensible to them, and he imagined that every subsequent year the Mayflower passengers must have resolved the previous winter was an aberration, and next year would be more hospitable.

But Israel Brewster was joyful. He was an ordained minister in the service of the Almighty in the rapidly growing township of Middleborough. He was madly in love, and today was the day his child would come. He knew there was always some element of doubt, but the midwife was making preparations, and Sarah seemed confident. Brewster knew he would meet his first child today.

His first child! Would it be a bubbly, mischievous son, or a tiny, beautiful daughter? After great debate the names had been resolved. A strapping young boy would be named after his Uncle Jonathan, and a delicate flower would be named after his Aunt Patience. Jonathan or Patience? Patience or Jonathan? He swung his axe in reckless abandon. He was so excited he might split enough wood for the entire colony.

Although he was still not a father, Brewster was already prepared with a smattering of toys, many of which he had proudly fashioned himself. Dolls were quite easy, but he could never emulate the beauty of the professionally made dolls from England, and one was at the ready. The whirligigs on a string were also quite easy, and through it would be years before the child could manipulate one, Brewster imagined the look of glee and astonishment as he tightened the string and the disc furiously spun. As he thought about the child's eyes lighting with wonder, he tried to fathom what color eyes the child would have. Would they be blue like his, or would the child inherit Sarah's delightful brown eyes? He could scarcely contain himself.

The midwife maintained a face of somber reserve throughout the previous weeks. She was young and inexperienced and expressed concern that, despite her best efforts, the child had not "flipped" properly in the womb. The Brewsters expected a more seasoned midwife to arrive from Plimoth this week, but in all likelihood she would not be arriving in Middleborough due to the forbidding weather. Still, Brewster approached this glorious day with his usual energy. He mentally lingered on the book of Isaiah and dreamed of that miraculous day more than sixteen hundred years ago:

"For unto us a child is born, unto us a son is given; and the government shall be upon his shoulder, and his name shall be called Wonderful, Counsellor, The mighty God, The everlasting Father, The Prince of Peace."

He had built an excessive fire inside the home, so warm he could probably roast a ham from outside the front door. He had boiled water, he had procured blankets, and he had sung to Sarah from outside the room. He had done all the extraneous things his nervous energy compelled him to do, as the scene of the birth was no place for a man. And rightfully so, as the moans and shrieks grew in quantity and volume as the evening progressed. At one point the shrieking reached such a feverish crescendo Brewster was certain he would either force himself into the room, or abscond to the next town.

The hours wore on, and Brewster could not possibly cut any more wood, or boil any more water, or fashion any more whirligigs. Finally, the shrieking began to dissipate, and Brewster was certain it was replaced by glorious new shrieking. Had the blessed moment arrived, or were his ears deceiving him? Brewster could not be more relieved when the midwife emerged.

The fire and candlelight illuminated the modest home, and the midwife's face was immersed in shadows. Brewster could still discern, however, an expression of inconsolable sadness accentuated with intense horror. She did not know whether to apologize, cry, or scream. Her eyes welled with tears as she covered her mouth and ran from the home. Brewster was grimly aware his home was now silent.

In the dim, flickering light was Sarah. Her breathing was labored, and Brewster could scarcely recognize her she looked so exhausted. Cradled in her arms was a tiny, blue creature who was destined to be little Patience Brewster. She was destined to cradle her doll from England, to wear ribbons in her hair, and to follow her mother everywhere. But Patience Brewster would be doing none of these things as she was stillborn.

Brewster feared he would collapse from the grief. He attempted to breathe and was not certain he could. Stillborn. One of the most unquestionable manifestations of divine wrath had arrived in his home. And it was all his fault.

He yearned to hold Sarah's hand and gaze into her eyes. He was a husband, a tough, hardened man of the New England frontier, and an influential minister. He would comfort his beloved. He would offer divine, holy truths of love and healing, and she would persevere. They would persevere. Instead he began to sob.

In his devastated state he had scarcely noticed how weary his beloved was. She was hardly conscious. He called her name, but he didn't believe she had heard. He roused her gently, but she did not seem responsive. He shook her more violently, and she finally turned to him and gazed upon him with her brown eyes that somehow lit the darkness. She looked at him one last time and with her final mortal breath, quietly and slowly uttered, "How blessed I have been."

After Brewster finally resigned himself to the fact that additional shaking and screaming would have no effect, he collapsed to the floor. He had no consolation to offer himself, for he knew. Oh, how he knew. He knew he was a wretched, miserable sinner in the eyes of heaven, and deserved no blessings or comfort from this life. He stared at the bed and could scarcely fathom the cosmic irony. For Israel Brewster had served in the militia, and Israel Brewster had been to Boston.

Israel Brewster was performing his duties with the militia of the United Colonies of New England in June 1660. He was seventeen years old, and his duties included guarding the prisoner. The horrible, reprehensible, blasphemous prisoner who was so opposed to the righteous work of the Almighty that the entire colony knew of her witchcraft. Thanks to the unyielding fervor of Governor Winthrop, decades prior to her final execution, at the height of her unrepentant apostasy, her monster of a stillborn child had been unearthed and its deformities exposed. There could be no further doubt of her wickedness.

The governor mercifully banned her from the society of good and righteous people for her vile heresies. But in a mania of unholy delusion, she returned time and again to Massachusetts Bay over the decades, spreading her deplorable heresy. The governor had no choice but to finally order her execution, and Israel Brewster was there. He and his militia compatriots escorted her from her cell. He stood silently by the elm tree on the "neck" of the city, south of the Boston Common on that summer day. And he was full of doubts.

He did not comprehend how this elegant, articulate woman could be a threat to John Winthrop and the elect. He did not understand or believe that a deformed, unborn child could be evidence of Satanic activity. He thought it was not Christian that this woman should be sentenced to die, because she believed in the "Antinomian heresy" and was therefore opposed to the law. Brewster's mind wandered, and he dwelled on Jesus Christ ending the stoning of the adulteress.

But the cowardly Brewster did nothing. He said nothing. She even looked him in the eye while enroute to the elm tree, and in a spate of conformity, he returned a malicious, spiteful stare. He stood a little straighter in his uniform, and did his best to look righteous as the noose was tightened. As she violently swung, her tortured, lifeless face burned into Brewster's consciousness, and the memory of Mary Dyer's execution would haunt his days. And now, nine years later, on a bitterly cold November day in a tiny bedroom in Middleborough, fate had claimed its terrible vengeance.

The trees had stopped spinning and Brewster could discern Wawetseka's remarkable face. She had been obviously sobbing, and he was uncertain if her hands had ever left his temples. She cast her eyes upward to the sky, and chanted in words unknowable to Brewster. And then he saw it. For years afterward he would deny to himself that he ever saw it, and if he did, it was certainly a shameful hallucination triggered by the mysterious hot brew. But on that day, while lying on his back in the forest, he saw a cloud.

Cloud was never quite the right description. Brewster witnessed a gray mist, or perhaps a miasma. He was certain it emanated from his mouth and nostrils, and it hovered and lingered over him in a shapeless form, perhaps two feet wide. Inside of it he was certain he could make out a hangman's noose, which then morphed into the shape of an infant. And the cloud rose. It ascended upward until it was out of reach, and it continued its ascent past the mighty trees. It seemed to break apart as it reached the sky, and Brewster breathed deeply.

For in a way he could never quite fathom, and due to a service he could never adequately repay, Israel Brewster was healed.

CHAPTER TEN

MIDDLEBOROUGH

Israel Brewster rose to his feet. He was groggy, thirsty, and confused. His head ached, and he was contemplating how to vomit in the most graceful fashion possible. He felt absolutely dreadful, but he somehow felt reborn. The feeling was like nothing he had ever known, and despite his mild physical maladies, a peaceful serenity engulfed him.

Wawetseka had composed herself and rose from the ground. She handed Brewster his shirt, and he noticed the elder powwas was nowhere to be found. After his shirt was on, she took his hand and led him out of the woods. Brewster spied a black-throated blue warbler perched above them, and its sharp, staccato song rang up in notes of five. He felt like he might be floating.

As they emerged from the woods the missionary activity was winding down, and the congregation was packing and preparing for the journey home. Wawetseka released his hand and held her own hand to his cheek.

"I know your pain and your pain was great, Two Ponds. I pray your spirit is free. Thank you for bringing your holy English wisdom to us today. You have much to offer us, and we much to offer you. We shall meet again." Without another word, she was gone.

How long was he indisposed? Based on the position of the sun, he guessed the entire endeavor took less than two hours, perhaps three. Brewster ignored any probing stares and promptly ascertained that despite his mid-afternoon absence, the day was a tremendous success. Bibles were distributed, prayers were taught, goods were traded, and Brewster was confident at least a dozen natives were on the path to Christian baptism. He assisted with closing prayers and made preparations for the journey home.

He was saddened to notice Alice had ridden ahead with Reverend Phelps and some others, and any efforts to ride ahead to catch her would appear unseemly. He checked his saddle bag to ensure he had not forgotten the herbs that he promised to procure for the Farwells. Even without the company of Alice, Brewster still enjoyed the journey home, with ample time to discuss woodworking with Reddington the carpenter.

The ensuing week was rainy, but Brewster's spirit was buoyant. How could he not be joyous? Summer had arrived and Middleborough was optimistic about this year's crops. His incessant night terrors had vanished. He received correspondence from Reverend Eliot and Reverend Mather thanking and congratulating him for leading the missionary effort. His Sunday sermon on the Biblical mandate for forgiveness was impactful and thoughtful. And finally, summer was the best time for courting.

Israel Brewster and Alice Fuller enjoyed several brief social encounters. They took walks, and Brewster was a regular mealtime guest at the Fuller home. It was clear, however, Alice remained aloof and their relationship had regressed since the event at Richmond Pond. Was she jealous of Wawetseka? Did she really believe the Reverend Brewster was capable of some tawdry, sinful encounter in the woods?

Brewster decided the only path forward was candor. He was indeed serious about this lovely creature, and his recent spiritual cleansing reinforced his inclination for another marriage, a scenario he would have thought impossible a mere six months ago. Was the time right to take their relationship to a deeper level?

During a picnic lunch on a perfect day, Brewster decided the time was right and it was also time for an accounting of the events at Richmond Pond. Alice seemed to be in a playful mood, and teased him about his mighty wrestling prowess. He abandoned any of the cold formality he would frequently be compelled to employ as a clergyman, and he was forthright and direct.

He reminisced about Sarah, and he recounted one of the darkest nights a human being could imagine. He conveyed his remarkable conversation with Linto, perhaps the most astute and curious native he had ever met. And after careful consideration, he revealed the events in Boston eleven years ago, including his subsequent obsessive guilt, the incessant nightmares, and the otherworldly Wampanoag healing ceremony. He had never been this candid with anyone but Sarah, and the honesty felt good. Alice seemed to fight back tears during the most intense recollections, and tightly held his hand. Any misunderstandings about Richmond Pond were quickly allayed.

In the ensuing days, the courtship appeared to be progressing well. The summer heat lent itself to cool drinks and an occasional, innocent rendezvous in a shady meadow or by a picturesque stream. Hands were held, hair was stroked, and affectionate feelings were conveyed. As the month progressed, however, Brewster became painfully aware of a horrific, unsettling development so unexpected and so revolting that he could scarcely fathom it.

Brewster had a competitor.

In hindsight, he should not have been surprised that such a lovely New England flower as Alice Fuller would catch the eye of other gentlemen, among them Reverend Phelps. He should not have been surprised that a mutual indulgence of delightfully glazed apples, and a long ride home together from Taunton in the cool of the evening would lead to the possibility of more. Glazed apples, indeed. They were probably decadently spiced with cinnamon. Brewster should have known better.

And so, it was in the summer of 1671 that the good and Godly citizens of Middleborough were treated to the spectacle of two ordained ministers vying for the affections of a young lady. Reverend Phelps, although geographically centered to the east in Plimoth, was not without his advantages. His remarkable crown of wavy blonde hair kept many a female parishioner fixated with rapt attention, even during the most tedious dissertations and pulpit lamentations. His voice was melodious and his smile was warm. He owned and played the violin marvelously, and the joyous sound of a duet with the harpsichord emanated from the Fuller home on several evenings, and the glorious, enchanting music filled Brewster with utter disgust. And worst of all, he was from one of the most prosperous families in Plimoth.

Brewster agonized over his quandary and paced in his home as if he were Cromwell planning the next Roundhead triumph. Should he compose a sonnet? Should he learn violin? How long would that take? Could Phelps recite the Kings of Israel and Judah in chronological order as he could? Maybe that would impress Alice.

The battle raged on for days, and then a week, and then a second week, and the people of Middleborough feared for their local champion. Reverend Phelps seemed to have the looks, the talent, the family name, and a sense of grace and decorum that made even the most rugged farmwoman swoon. Brewster was so distracted he almost forgot his commitment to Reverend Mather, and almost forgot to attend the next scheduled meeting of the Plimoth General Court.

Fortunately, he did not forget, and once again, he and Brownie had a shared destination. Brewster couldn't be entirely certain, but it seemed increasingly evident Brownie was growing more insubordinate and flatulent with each new journey, and he increasingly grew to understand why the township was so amenable to lending her out at any time whatsoever.

Brewster donned his most appropriate attire and rode east. The memory of his public reprimand at the hands of

Jeremiah Barron was lingering, and Brewster resolved to not speak unless spoken to. As the preliminary mingling wound down, he was surprised to see his brother in Christ, but adversary in romance, approach him.

"Reverend Brewster! Blessings upon you, sir. Greetings in the name of the risen Lord!"

Brewster quickly evaluated his options. He contemplated silently and icily ignoring him. He contemplated springing into action with the vaunted wrestling move utilized to swiftly render Linto helpless. He was disappointed, however, when he realized he would meekly employ his third option.

"Reverend Phelps, I am indeed blessed to be in the presence of this august body once again. Blessings upon you and your family, sir."

"It is indeed fortuitous that you are present, Reverend Brewster, as I understand the court wishes to formally recognize your recent actions. They were contemplating sending a messenger, but they hoped you would come on your own volition."

"Indeed? Well, it is fortuitous, indeed." Finally. Finally, the diligent and humble Israel Brewster would receive some formal recognition for his works for the Lord and for the colony. The day at Richmond Pond was a tremendous success, and many natives were subsequently baptized as Christians. Brewster wondered what impact his revelation about Wamsutta had on the Wampanoag, but he strongly suspected that due to Linto and the mission visit, he was single-handedly responsible for tremendously defraying the tensions reverberating through the land.

The assembly was called to order and as usual, earnest and solemn prayer was the first priority. After imploring the Almighty for strength and guidance in the face of the savages, Governor Prence outlined the agenda.

"King Philip" was still foremost on the minds of the

government. During a secret, closed-door session in the last week, the Sachem was finally held to account. Although initially denying his hostile schemes, he was soon confronted with undeniable evidence. The evidence was procured and supplied surreptitiously by the colony's vast Christian network of informants living among the various Indian nations. Assistant Governor Winslow was practically smirking as the governor recounted the event. A clearly unsettled and discouraged "King Philip" could no longer deny his wrongdoing, and he had acquiesced. He had admittedly engaged in unlawful treachery, and he had agreed the Wampanoag would surrender their firearms. The chamber was elated and buzzed with reserved but unmistakable huzzahs.

The details of how and when the firearms would be seized were discussed at length, and Brewster, as one who lived and ministered so close to the Wampanoag, knew he should be pleased with the news of a disarmed adversary. But as he searched his heart, he only felt a sense of strange ambivalence. His mind labored so intently on the issue that he failed to hear that he was being addressed.

After a gentle nudging from a neighbor, the Reverend Brewster stood, waiting to receive his accolades and contemplating his address to the chamber. He would certainly thank Reverend Eliot as well as his congregation. Should he mention Alice? She might relish news of her being praised at the General Court, but he did not wish to generate jealousy among all the other townspeople who did so very much at Richmond Pond. Finally, he was directed to come forward and stand before the assembly. It was, much to his disappointment, Jeremiah Barron who was leading the proceedings. The screeching began.

Jeremiah Barron was in a fine mood and was resplendent in a new cloak from England. He had been eating and living well, as his new African servant girl had been seeing to all of his worldly needs. Once again, like an actor stepping onto the stage, he stood and cast his glare on Brewster.

"Reverend Israel Brewster of Middleborough, you stand before this court to answer for some inexplicably questionable behavior you have allegedly engaged in during these previous weeks. Do you have any opening remarks?" Brewster was so taken aback he stood before the court perplexed and dumbfounded. He did not speak a word.

"Very well. The first matter is relatively inconsequential, but I find it to be most unsettling indeed. Is this court to understand that in recent days, while entrusted to lead your congregation at a Christian missionary service among the heathen, that you, an ordained minister of Christ's holy church, did cast off all the civilized decorum that should be expected of you, and in a state of half-naked mania, actually wrestle with the savages?" There were some quiet but audible gasps as Brewster did not deny the accusation, and even had the audacity to brag that he was victorious in one bout but still harbored deep suspicions his opponent threw the match. His levity was not well received.

"Reverend Brewster, I am uncertain about any implications of *illegality* in this affair." Barron paused to accentuate the word as if it was a sacred piece of prophecy from a Hebrew scroll. "But it is clear to me and this General Court that the conduct was buffoonish and not at all commensurate with a learned Christian reverend. Unfortunately, there are numerous other concerns.

"The Court has it on good authority that while engaged with the savages near Taunton, you did, intentionally and willfully, procure a pagan intoxicant of some mysterious form in order to encourage lustful deeds for a member of your flock." Brewster was genuinely flabbergasted, and could not comprehend what Barron was accusing him of. He pled ignorance.

Jeremiah Barron became so animated and screechy that Brewster thought he might take to the air and fly away. "How dare you! How dare you claim ignorance in these matters when the testimony and evidence is so clear! Did you, or did you not, procure from the savages a filthy, sinful weed which goes by the name of Summer Savory, and encourage, in the name of holy and Christian counseling, a member of your flock to consume it? Answer the question, Reverend!"

Brewster's confusion was eliminated and he actually smiled, clearly enraging his inquisitor even more. He patiently and helpfully explained the harmless and medicinal properties of Summer Savory and its utility in healthful Christian marriage. Barron would not be placated, and Brewster was stunned to hear a voice, almost certainly Reverend Phelps, bellow, "Shame! Shame I say!"

Barron was in the full throes of his glorious performance, and much to Brewster's horror, he was just warming up. "Reverend, I must say, I am astounded that your childish, shirtless buffoonery and your embrace of herbal witchcraft actually pale in comparison to subsequent accounts. For this next discussion, I must caution the chambers be cleared of any young, innocent children." Barron could clearly see there were, and almost never were, any children in the chamber, but he relished the drama.

"Israel Brewster!" Brewster had noticed Barron had ceased to address him as a reverend. "Israel Brewster, I am horrified to hear accounts that you willingly and voluntarily subjected yourself to pagan witchcraft at the hands of the savages, and devoured a vile, intoxicating brew. It seems that once again, you chose to gallivant among the savages in a half-naked, delirious state.

"How can a minister, a devout servant of Christ, expose himself to such wickedness? The fact that you would voluntarily consume this Satanic concoction, leads me to question your fitness as a clergyman!" The chamber was awash in increasingly audible gasps and whispers. Eyes dripping with malice and accusation now glowered at the miscreant standing before them. Brewster was uncertain if he was expected to answer, but he would have remained speechless regardless. He began to feel dizzy, and he also feared for the health of Jeremiah Barron, who seemed to be whipped into such a frenzy Brewster feared he may not survive to proffer additional accusations.

"And yet!" Barron paused to make a conscientious effort to quiet the chamber, most of whom were on the edge of their seats. "And yet, this man standing before us is reported to be guilty of even *more* blasphemy. There is reliable, yet stunning testimony, that Israel Brewster, charged with the proper and orthodox Christian education and indoctrination of his flock, when given the opportunity to be alone with impressionable young women, questioned the holy authority inherent in these colonies, and questioned the lawful and necessary execution of...*Mary Dyer?*"

Most of the chamber was standing now and Barron raged on. "Mary Dyer, the unrepentant, deceitful heretic of malicious thought and deed? Mary Dyer, the unceasing, unrepentant advocate of, of, of..." Brewster feared he would not be able to clearly hear Jeremiah Barron if his voice rose any higher. "The advocate of Quakerism? The woman whose wickedness was so clearly and unquestionably revealed by the birth of her stillborn..." Brewster's eyes closed.

"*Her satanic, stillborn monster!* What say you, Israel Brewster? How can you answer for your heresy?"

Brewster remained silent as his eyes welled with tears. He thought of that day with Alice, and he could see across the room, through his tears, the Reverend Phelps was no longer trying to conceal his smile. Barron proudly resumed his seat as if he had just slayed a hundred Philistines.

The stately and dignified Governor Prence was sadly shaking his head. Fearing his lack of composure, Winslow quickly took the lead. In the previous weeks, he had finally pieced together that this was the scrawny, timid militiaman who was with him during Wamsutta's final week.

"Israel Brewster, these accusations are most severe indeed. As the Assistant Governor, I am within my authority to make the following lawful and public declarations. First, you are immediately relieved of your duties to the church and congregation of your current posting. Secondly, you will immediately vacate the parsonage provided to you by the congregation. Thirdly, the Reverend Phelps is hereby named as the interim minister in the township of Middleborough. Finally, you will report back to this court in three days, so Plimoth Colony can fully evaluate the true nature of these heresies, and what, if any accomplices you may have conspired with.

"Since the Court recognizes your legal status as an ordained minister, and as a veteran who devoted honorable service to the militia of these United Colonies, you are hereby remanded to your own custody to take charge of your possessions, and to orchestrate your defense. May the Lord bless and protect Plimoth Colony."

Governor Prence subsequently conducted the remaining affairs of the court, and soon all were dismissed. Brewster staggered outside in a state of apoplectic shock. He made eye contact with no one, but was certain he was being carefully watched.

Brownie could somehow ascertain that she transported an ebullient, energetic servant of the Lord to Plimoth, and returned with a broken, dispirited shell of a man. The ride to Middleborough was plodding and grueling. One might think Brewster was not even on the mare, as Brownie seemed to find her own way.

Brewster had no doubt the news of his disgrace travelled to Middleborough quicker than Brownie ever could. He rode through the town, once again aware of the curious glares that his eyes would not meet. He dismounted at home.

This was the home he had known for years. It was Sarah's home, and, yes, it was the home of Patience Brewster. Brewster gathered a mug of small beer and collapsed into a chair. He mentally began to plot his defense. The treachery and lies of Phelps. The efficacy and beauty of the healing ceremony. Mary Dyer had been gone for years and the Quaker threat had been extinguished.

He would confer with Reverend Mather. Certainly, John Eliot would testify on his behalf. And Alice. Sweet, innocent Alice. How cruelly she had been manipulated by that reprobate Phelps. Perhaps they would even hear testimony from Linto? Yes, yes. This was shaping up magnificently. They would regret their actions. Brewster would be wise, articulate and passionate. He was a righteous man who trusted in the Lord. He closed his eyes and contemplated the eighth chapter of the book of Romans:

"What shall we then say to these things? If God be for us, who can be against us?"

Indeed. Brewster began to pace and the excitement was building. Soon that smug Jeremiah Barron would have his comeuppance. Brewster began rummaging through his library in search of the tomes he would require to orchestrate his defense. He set one book aside and then another. He searched through his desk drawers. And Brewster paused.

Brewster paused, because almost inadvertently, he had found in his trembling hand, another of Sarah's hand-written love sonnets:

"What manner a man, bold, right and brave
Who defends the truth, with dignity and might
A man strong and righteous, he a wife will crave
The servant of the Lord, tasked to shine his light.
What manner of a man, weak, small afraid?

Who hates the other and hides himself away
A man of dishonor, the work of God betrayed
The devout flee his side, and yet the wicked stay.
I, a humble wife have made my choice clear
In a fallen wicked world I have the strength to face
Through holy matrimony and devout Christian cheer
My Israel is my strength, and his side is my place.
How blessed I have been*, to hold such a hand*
Husband and wife forever, God's will has been planned."

Brewster fell to his chair and re-read the sonnet three times. The emotions surged though him, and he furiously scoured the house. He gathered her letters, her sonnets, and the lock of her hair. He gathered his grandfather's book and his father's Bible. He managed to find a loaf of bread, and a wheel of cheese. Brewster chaotically threw shirts, breeches, stockings, shoes, and buckles into a satchel. For Israel Brewster was leaving.

He left the door to the home ajar, secured his possessions tightly to Brownie, and was soon atop his companion. He had nothing in this world but his books and memories, some modest clothes, a day's worth of food, and a flatulent, slow, insubordinate mare. But the Reverend Israel Brewster was leaving, and that was all that mattered.

He mentally plotted the route to Plimoth, and he pointed Brownie in the opposite direction.

CHAPTER ELEVEN

MONTAUP

Metacomet stared into the fire. He felt lost and alone. He had prayed throughout the day, and desperately tried to commune with Wamsutta. Linto had offered to sit by the fire with him, but the Sachem promptly sent him away.

What had he done? He had saved the future of the Wampanoag, and fulfilled his sacred responsibility as Sachem. What else could he have done?

Metacomet was mentally reliving the events of that summer. It was four moons ago from this day, and the talk of war was incessant. The firearms were stockpiled, but there were more to be had. They would get them from the Dutch if need be, or the Abenaki would get them from the French, but they would get them somehow. The nations were preparing. Weetamoo was preparing to dismiss her lackey of a husband and his English sympathies (how sad a fate to be tied to such a man after being married to his brother). The Wampanoag were obsessively watching villages, forts and armories, always probing, and taking stock of the English weaknesses. Tobias was sharpening his long knives.

They were ready to avenge the injustices visited upon them. They would govern the land as they saw fit. And Skunk Genitals the murderer would pay dearly for his wretched poison. But Metacomet was still wrought with doubt and indecision.

Betraying the alliance his father built fifty summers ago would be devastating. Even worse, Metacomet knew all too well how vicious these English could be when threatened, despite all the talk of love and peace in their big, ancient book. The Pequot certainly learned that lesson, shortly before

Metacomet was born. Now hundreds of them were in bondage across the sea.

Metacomet had incessantly pleaded with his ancestors and the heavens for divine guidance during those days.

But then came Linto. Breathless, exhausted Linto. He had rowed his mashoon furiously south on the river the English called Tawntawn or some hideous thing, instead of its proper name. Metacomet feared Linto would lose consciousness after the sprint to Montaup, and he forced him to rest and breathe before addressing him.

"It has happened, Sachem. The Great Spirit has blessed me. I finally have something to say. I can finally serve you as it was meant to be."

Linto recounted his extraordinary encounter with the Englishman he called Two Ponds. Metacomet was inclined to believe it was all an elaborate English hoax, and he thought long and hard about finding this Two Ponds and staring into his soul. But this was Linto. Miraculous Linto, the hope of his people.

"Sachem, his words were astounding. Every word, just as Mentayyup recounted. He was there at the hunting camp. He knew every detail. He was one of the two frightened rabbits! There was no physic potion or whatever they called it. He saw Wamsutta throw it into the woods. Wamsutta never took anything from Winslow! And Two Ponds received Wamsutta's dying words at Plimoth."

Metacomet's mind was in torment. Everything about these English was trickery and fraud. How could they formulate this deception? Whenever Metacomet had cause for suspicion, he somehow always gravitated to the pious Christian, Sassamon. Did Sassamon somehow tell the Two Ponds about Linto? Did the Two Ponds seek out Linto? Metacomet began to sweat profusely. And then Linto recited the words.

"You have offered me much but I have accepted nothing. You have seen this with your own eyes. Though my destiny is closed, my fault is with the heavens. I have not been corrupted or poisoned by the English. Ensure the people understand and bear no ill tidings."

Linto recited the words six times for Metacomet. They were recited twice in English, and Linto translated them to Metacomet's tongue and then repeated them four more times. Metacomet seemed to quiver during the last recital. He felt as if Wamsutta was addressing him from the spirit world. He fell to his knees and tried to breathe.

"My Sachem, Two Ponds tried to tell his superiors. You know how ignorant they can be. For all of these nine summers, Two Ponds had no idea what the words meant. They were burned into his memory but he paid them no mind."

It was a miracle, and the fact that Linto was the instrument of the miracle reinforced everything Metacomet had believed about him. Metacomet had finally been given his divine guidance.

In the ensuing days and weeks, Metacomet felt remorse that he was ready to slice Winslow's throat for a crime he was not guilty of. The heavens had spoken and now was not the time for war. Tobias and the young warriors could barely contain their fury, but that could not be helped. Weetamoo raged, but her husband congratulated Metacomet on his wisdom, and said he looked more like Massasoit every day. Sassamon was elated and praised his Christian God. But what to do with Plimoth?

Metacomet knew the English had ears everywhere, and he was not surprised when he was summoned to Plimoth soon after Linto's revelation. Had Metacomet not received Linto's testimony, he would (cognizant of Wamsutta's fate), probably have declined the summons, which in itself could have triggered war. But armed with Linto's miraculous truth, Metacomet would face his English friends, and all would be well once again.

Metacomet stood before Winslow and the ancient Prence in their hallowed Court. He was not treated as a

Sachem or as a friend, and the accusations and condescension came like repeated slaps to the cheek. But Metacomet would be patient and forgiving. What was it their crucified Son preached? Let them keep slapping you, your reward will be in the heavens.

Metacomet did his best to deny any talk of rebellion and treachery, and he was not entirely truthful. Clearly some degree of falsehood would be required to placate these Englishmen, some of whom seemed to want to crucify *him*. They addressed him as "Philip," and he shook his head and calmly denied the accusations.

But then came the evidence. What did they call it? Oh yes, corroboration. The accusations were *corroborated* by testimony. Metacomet listened, horrified, as his words and deeds came back to haunt him. His previous suspicions that Wamsutta was poisoned. His discussions with Weetamoo. His solicitations for more firearms. Metacomet knew the English listening network was very comprehensive, but he was absolutely stunned as his words and plans were recited verbatim. And he was cornered.

Mentayyup stood solemnly on his right, and Tobias stood on his left, shaking his head and growling, but he was cornered. And he agreed to their demands. He would see the Wampanoag stripped of their firearms. They were given two moons to comply, but they would comply. They would bring their guns to Tawntawn.

As the heat of the summer simmered, the Sachem of the Wampanoag could not bring himself to fulfill his commitment. There had to be way. Certainly, these men of Plimoth would come to their senses. How pathetic and defenseless his people would be without firearms, desperately dependent upon the English to defend them from any hostility. There simply had to be another path. And the proud Wampanoag did not appear in Tawntawn to relinquish their firearms.

Metacomet knew this action would cause turmoil but he needed time to think. Perhaps Linto would find another miracle. The men of Plimoth gave him twenty more sunrises to end his "insolent carriages," but Metacomet would find a way. Based on Linto's suggestion, Metacomet would plead his case to the other Englishmen. Perhaps the educated men of Boston, who were so wise and refined, and had such nice things, would understand how maliciously his people were being treated. Yes, the men of Boston would dispense justice.

Metacomet's words rang hollow in Boston, and he learned an Englishman was an Englishman whether they called themselves "Plimoth" or "Massachusetts Bay" or "New Haven" or anything else. He knew his incessant stalling would trigger rage in Skunk Genitals Winslow, but he saw little option. He knew going to speak with the refined men of Boston would cause trouble, but he had tried. He knew there was talk of war, and all the Englishmen in every direction were arming themselves to the teeth and standing shoulder to shoulder and marching up and down their streets. He would never understand their ways.

Metacomet resolved to remain on the path of peace, and there could be no more stalling. It was time to end the tension. They would have friendship with Plimoth. And so, four moons after Linto rushed up the hillside with the joyful news, Metacomet signed. He signed whatever the English put in front of him. And Mentayyup and Tobias and even Linto put their marks on the document. Of course, Sassamon was there to translate and ensure everything was in order.

The document was humiliating. Metacomet attested that he and all the Wampanoag were "subjects of his Majesty, the King of England" and "subject to the laws of Plimoth Colony." He was forced to promise to sell no land unless the ancient Prence said it was acceptable. If he was not humiliated enough, he agreed to pay one hundred pounds worth of goods within three years in order to compensate the government for the trouble he created. And as the final dagger, in a clause that added no value except further submission, a clause that Skunk Genitals demanded be part of the agreement, he was to bring Plimoth five wolf heads every year.

But it was done. He had maintained the blessed friendship his father had been so proud of. There would be peace, and the Wampanoag would not walk the path of the Pequot. He stirred the fire and prayed his actions were righteous, for as Sassamon bleated constantly, "blessed are the peacemakers." The face Metacomet now showed the world was a solemn testament to peace and brotherhood.

But inside, the Sachem's soul burned white hot with rage.

Part Two
1674

"And whereas they (The Wampanoag and Narragansett) have been quiet until the last year, that must be ascribed to the wonderful Providence of God, who did (as with Jacob of old, and after that, with the Children of Israel), lay the fear of the English, and the dread of them, upon all the Indians... *The terror of God was upon them round about.*"

- *Reverend Increase Mather 1676*

CHAPTER TWELVE
PROVIDENCE

Izzy did not know how much more he could take.

"Elah...Zimri...Omri..." The small crowd whooped with pleasure. Violent and sudden sickness was a distinct possibility. No, it was a distinct probability.

"Ahab, Ahaziah, Jeroram..." He was now being swung back and forth through the air, which was not part of the arrangement at all. He was ready to register a stern protest, but the ale was in his nostrils, and he had difficulty enunciating. He thought the better of his protest and resumed the task at hand.

"Jehu, Jehoahaz, Jehoash, Jeroboam..."

A critic shouted his denunciation. "You said Jeroboam already! Quit cheating, Izzy!"

"I meant Jeroboam the second, Zechariah, Shallum, Menahem, Pekahiah..." He closed his blue eyes and strained to recall. He was in trouble, as he could not remember the rest, and had no means to make good on the wager. Leveraging all his faculties, he persevered. "Pekah and Hoshea! Yes! Yes! And then the kingdom fell! Pay up, you scalawags! Rum for the house!" Izzy Brewster was triumphant.

He was socializing in a seedy tavern on the waterfront in Providence, in the Colony of Rhode Island. It was actually known as the Colony of Rhode Island and Providence Plantations, but at the moment he was not in a formal mood. His money, as usual, ran dry far before his craving for rum, and the situation required a creative solution. With no other discernible options, Izzy negotiated one of his classic tavern wagers. On this occasion, he wagered he could recite all the Kings of Israel. Correctly. In chronological order. While being held upside down by his ankles. While drinking a pint of ale. BUT, it should be noted, being swung in a circle while being marched through the tavern was NOT part of the negotiation.

After the rum was poured Izzy quickly and magnanimously forgave his enormous tormentor for his extracurricular swinging. Izzy was contemplating whether any other soul in the tavern could possibly confirm the accuracy of his recital. He had been tempted to insert King Blissandblas and King Rummydumdum after Jehu, but liquor was at stake, and he did not want to take any unnecessary chances.

Soon the commotion died down and Israel Brewster was sitting alone at a table and taking stock of his life. Less than four years ago, he was an ordained minister and an upstanding member of the holy Plimoth Colony. Now he was a member in good standing of the unwashed working class of Providence. As such, he could not bear to even hear or see his name anymore, and the world knew him as Izzy. Like the Kingdom of Israel, he was a broken, fallen, desolate institution and he wondered if he would see the day when some pagan enemy of God carried him away to bondage of some sort.

Still, as the rum settled his stomach, he convinced himself how pleased he was. He was certainly not the first colonist to be scorned and exiled by his righteous, Calvinist brethren. There was a certain freedom and excitement to Providence. He enjoyed his new vocation, because the world needed barrels (probably more than it needed spiritual guidance) and at age thirty-two, he was still the picture of health.

He was slowly coming to terms with the reality that, for a man destined to assemble barrels in six hours, he had probably consumed enough alcohol. He bid farewell to his newfound friends and staggered back to his one-room cabin, where he stared at his decrepit ceiling. And Izzy thought about Israel Brewster.

Was this his destiny? In hindsight, the notion and presumption that he was ever a member of God's chosen "elect" seemed almost uproarious. Was he eternally damned? Would he be eternally separated from Sarah? Could there be any salvation for a disgraced minister?

Perhaps his most compelling regret was the unseemly fleeing. The sudden, cowardly, unannounced absconding from Plimoth Colony and all he held dear. What would Winslow have done with him if he showed his face and mounted a vigorous defense? The outcome would certainly have been preordained, with plenty of leering and shouting from a Godly audience. Chains? The stockade? A public whipping?

Brewster genuinely believed Winslow retained a pang of admiration and sympathy for him, due to his status as a veteran of the militia. More specifically and endearing, he was a veteran of the great and holy campaign to drag the dangerous Wamsutta to Plimoth! Heaven be praised!

With or without a public whipping, the infamous Reverend Israel Brewster of Middleborough, he thought, was fated to be defrocked, disgraced, and exiled somewhere west of the colony with the rest of the unholy reprobates. Predestination was a cruel thing, indeed.

Izzy Brewster fell unconscious while deliberating the cosmic mystery of fate. Soon the sunlight burst through his room, and he managed to compose himself adequately to wash his face, devour a plate of day-old stew, and climb aboard his only friend in New England.

The temptation to sell Brownie hung over Brewster relentlessly these past three years. From a legal perspective, he wasn't even certain if he "owned" her. Was she still on loan from the congregation? Perhaps he should consider her as a farewell gift? Or did she embody his newfound renegade status as the defrocked clergyman raging against the injustice of Plimoth Colony aboard his ill-gotten, four-legged contraband?

Regardless of how he construed their relationship, a quick and easy sale would have been most conducive to elevating his situation in some meager fashion. She certainly ate a lot, perhaps more than he did. He really had no concrete need for transportation, as his work was less than two miles away from his cabin, and equally important, so were the taverns. And although he had never taken a vow of poverty, he may as well have, as that is where his life had led, and compensation for the sale of a horse would have been welcome.

He had never taken a vow of celibacy either, but, as with the poverty, some things seem to be preordained. Of course, few gentlemen prospects could cause a maiden's heart to flutter quite like an impoverished, defrocked minister who owned a flatulent horse and was a passable cooper, but there was no accounting for taste. He often felt the temptation of the tawdry and lascivious wenches of the taverns, but for better or worse, a life as an ordained minister and the eternal memory of Sarah rendered him undesirous of such a course.

Brewster's spirit was still lofty, however, as he mounted Brownie and greeted the day. His head pounded, and he made a note that being suspended by his ankles for prolonged periods was not a proven remedy to mitigate the agony of prolific rum consumption. His aroma seemed to horrify and disappoint Brownie, who snorted her stern reprimand.

Soon he was at the cooperage, and Mister Barlow pretended not to notice his late arrival. In an age of wickedness and shiftlessness, Barlow was pleased to have an employee who came to work on a generally regular basis and performed outstanding work. When Brewster presented himself to volunteer his services three years ago, Barlow initially insisted on a formal apprenticeship, but Brewster would have none of it because after recent events, seven years seemed like a lifetime. Barlow relented and was rewarded for his flexibility, for Izzy Brewster was remarkably diligent, studious, and polite and soon became a valuable asset.

    Izzy often wondered why he had stumbled into the profession. He had thought long and hard about taking to sea, but the reality was, despite a lifetime lived in New England, he had never even set foot on a boat, and he wasn't sure doing so was such a good idea. Besides, who would take care of Brownie?

    Was he drawn to the legend of John Alden, coopering on the Mayflower and heroically bringing God's light to the wilderness alongside Grandfather Brewster? Alden quickly made the colossal leap from cooper to acting governor. Perhaps that was in the stars for him as well? Sometimes his mind wandered to Joshua Farwell who was also a cooper. Brewster often wondered if his marriage counseling had done even the slightest good, and if the vile and wicked Summer Savory had any efficacy in the matter.

    He quietly focused on his work. He was still a "slack" cooper who was limited to products containing dry goods only. Without a formal apprenticeship, it would be difficult to progress to the status of "tight" cooper, commissioned to construct barrels that were sound enough to hold liquid. It was just as well, for as Mister Barlow reminded him, Izzy had probably seen enough barrels full of liquid when away from the cooperage.

    Brewster set his mind to turning out eight pine barrels on that day. He marveled that a mere four years ago, the verbiage associated with his profession included "salvation, sin, predestination, and resurrection," whereas now his daily work focused on "staves, quarter-hoops, bilges and rivets." He was focused on shaping the interior angles of the staves of his first barrel using his drawknife and trusty "shaving horse." Across the room, Mister Barlow had a customer.

The customer seemed well-to-do and Barlow addressed him in the obsequious manner he utilized when it was clear a gentleman had the means and the need to procure dozens of barrels. He was modestly dressed in the style associated with the faithful of Providence, and Izzy surmised he was probably a Quaker. He negotiated his business with Mister Barlow in a courteous and direct manner. Just when he seemed to be on verge of finalizing the procurement of thirty various barrels for a business venture, he stopped speaking. He glared across the room at the cooper who was fixated on his work and paying him no mind. The gentleman's expression became quizzical and he seemed slightly perturbed. "You there! You!"

	Brewster found it inconceivable anyone would have a reason to address him, and he silently contemplated his staves. The gentleman suddenly stormed away from his negotiations with Barlow and cornered him.

	Barlow followed, elevating his obsequiousness to greater heights. He blinked repeatedly and stammered. "G-G-Governor Easton, I am certain whatever mischief this workman has done, he will be held to account! I j-j-just hope any unsavory acts on his part will not infringe upon our business dealings. Brewster! Stand up when you're addressed, Izzy!"

	Brewster rose to his feet and the stranger glowered at him. "Brewster! You were the center of attention in the tavern last night, were you not? What a buffoon you are, young man. I am amazed you have found the stamina to perform your duties today! I am Deputy Governor John Easton."

	Brewster stood in stunned silence. When he was a devout, pious minister, he seemed to be incessantly reprimanded by a deputy or assistant governor of some sort. Now that he lived in a different colony and was a tavern clown, here he was being reprimanded by the deputy governor. He wondered if there were any other colonies in New England that would take him in.

He concluded honesty and respect would be the most logical course at the moment. "Aye, Governor. It was I, partaking a bit too much of the devil's brew. I do apologize if any of my behavior was unseemly."

"Brewster…Brewster. IZZY? ISRAEL? Israel Brewster? An ordained minister?"

Brewster's cheeks felt hot and flush and he stared at the ground. Mister Barlow's mouth was agape. "Aye, sir. That was years ago. Why would you know of me, Governor?"

"Young man, we here in Providence remain well informed of the dissenters and exiles migrating from our Puritan brothers northeast of here. I know of you, and I know of the accusations against you. It was three or four years ago, I believe?"

Mister Barlow sensed a threat to his transaction and had fortunately stopped his stammering. "Governor, I assure you, I had no idea this man was in trouble. I have no idea what manner of accusations have been leveled against this…this…*workman.*"

"Mister Barlow, the Israel Brewster I knew was renowned in this colony for his dignity and righteousness in bringing the holy light of Christ to our neighbors, the Indians. The fact he was scorned and reviled by his government is a travesty."

Barlow nodded as if his head was on a hinge. "Governor, I couldn't agree more. A travesty, a complete travesty it was."

Deputy Governor Easton rolled his eyes. "Young Brewster, my friends and I were in the tavern, searching out lost and troubled souls. It would appear as if, praise God, we have found one. I am requesting your company as my personal guest for Christian worship tomorrow. Seven in the morning at the meeting house three blocks north of here."

Brewster recognized the place. He turned away and was barely audible. "You want me to be a Quaker."

"*I want you to stop being a drunken ass, Israel Brewster!*" Easton's voice was so forceful the barrel staves appeared to quiver. "And you will be my personal guest!"

"Governor, I know you are kind, and your intentions are true. But frankly, I'm not sure church attendance is mandatory in the colony, and tomorrow is the day I sleep. A lot."

Easton remained silent and took a deep breath. "Barlow! I am saddened to remove a talented cooper from your employ, but do you have any idea of the severe criminal penalty for one who ridicules the Bible in a public place, especially a tavern? Do you?"

The stammer returned. "N-N-No."

"Neither do I. But as the Deputy Governor, I have all day to invent a penalty. So, one way or another, I will see you again, Israel Brewster. Good day. Oh, and Barlow! Make it forty barrels. It's much more Biblical."

"Y-Yes sir, Governor. Yes sir."

CHAPTER THIRTEEN

MONTAUP

Linto was uncomfortable.

He was fatigued, that much was certain. Over the summer his son went from crawling, to frantically walking and making mischief. His daughter, still an infant, was crying through the night. He thought long and hard about being wed to one of the most remarkable healers in all the nations, yet enduring constant sleep deprivation because the child was too unhealthy to sleep. He stood and vigorously rubbed his eyes.

Outside the wetu, he could hear Tobias and his son Wampapaquan laughing with their rollicking dice game. Mentayyup was playing too, along with Wampapaquan's friend Mattashunnamo. Mentayyup, however, always being solemn and dignified, left the game when the stakes began to get, as he put it, "unhealthy."

Linto did not see Wampapaquan often, and when he did, he was usually astounded by his height and maturity. It seemed inconceivable that Tobias' son was reaching manhood, and yet there he was, only five or six summers younger than Linto. It also seemed inconceivable that Linto was now an exhausted father of two, but time marches quickly.

In recent years, Tobias, Wampapaquan, and Mattashunnamo had become an inseparable trio. They seemed to share a love of hunting, archery, gambling, and liquor, and they also shared a mutual disdain for the English and the Christians.

Consequently, the festivities were especially delightful for the trio, as they were making a mockery of Patuckson, who was a devoted companion of Sassamon and an English-loving Christian. When they threw dice, they took his money. When they arm-wrestled, they took his money. When they flipped coins, they took his money. As the afternoon progressed, they seemed to be inventing new, unprecedented ways to gamble and take his money.

Amidst jovial laughter, they demanded to know if the English God intended to intervene in order to save His devotee from further humiliation. Patuckson was not laughing at all, as he was now seriously in debt to Tobias, and more importantly, he would not tolerate blasphemy.

Linto overheard all the tumult while he was trying to work. Although still relatively young, Linto knew nothing good ever came from too much gambling. He also thought Christians were not supposed to gamble. When he asked Sassamon about it last month, he replied with nothing but a shrug.

Linto often wished he could ask Two Ponds these things, as there was no other Christian he trusted so much, but no one had heard a thing from him in years. Many Englishmen told Linto that Two Ponds had somehow disgraced himself, and he ran away in shame. A farmer in Taunton said he went to England and now serves in the cavalry. Some even said he perished from fever. Linto was saddened by the thought.

In addition to the discomfort generated by Sassamon's friend Patuckson, Sassamon himself was causing Linto grave discomfort. He was away in Plimoth discussing land transactions, and in his absence, Metacomet surreptitiously asked Linto to review some Wampanoag legal documents written in English. Due to his remarkable English skills, Sassamon handled all of these issues for the Sachem and the Wampanoag. He was the Sachem's liaison to the mysterious world of Plimoth Colony.

Sassamon would obviously be offended at the prospect, but Metacomet demanded it be done, and he was convinced Linto was up to the task. Although Linto had previously spoken English relatively well, during the last three years or so he had studiously focused on reading and writing it. He attended more missionary services, and he read the Bible frequently. He exchanged correspondence with Englishmen in Taunton (at least those willing to write). As far as he knew, only the Sachem and Wawetseka knew of his impressive proficiency.

Despite Linto's familiarity with the English Bible he still, much to the grave disappointment of Sassamon and Reverend Eliot, had not been baptized as a Christian, and he wondered if he ever would. The heavy-handed ways of Plimoth had soured him over the previous years, and he felt like he would never be able to overcome his doubts and confusion.

Last night he was reading in the Bible that God did not want His people to plant their fields with two different types of seed, or wear clothes made from two different types of materials. Why would God care about such things? Every single person in Linto's village perished from the plague, and these are the things God cares about? Why did he tell the people in Israel they could not eat lobster? Linto could not imagine trying to get through a winter without lobster.

Nothing was getting any easier with the English, and he wished again that Two Ponds could be there to help him understand. He was never condescending and rude like so many of the others. Two Ponds never told Linto he was a "savage." Linto thought everything would be better once Metacomet signed the document of peace three years ago, but still Plimoth treated them with contempt. Linto suspected the Sachem was scheming with Weetamoo and the Narragansett again, but he could not be certain. Metacomet did not share these things with him.

So Linto was unsettled on that November day, and winter would arrive very soon. He considered putting his head down for a nap, but the more legal documents he perused, the more agitated he became. Clearly something was not right.

A parcel of land east of Montaup, near the village of Acushnet was sold in the spring. Linto recalled Sassamon clearly told Metacomet the English would pay ten cooking pots, ten axes, twenty knives, and twenty wool coats. But according to this document signed with the official seal of Plimoth, the agreed compensation was fifteen pots, twelve axes, twenty-five knives, and twenty coats. Where did the extra pots, axes, and knives go?

The more Linto probed, the more horrified he was. On almost every legally sanctioned land transaction in the last five years, Sassamon had found a way to lie and deceive using the language barrier. His illicit profiteering was staggering. What was even more shocking, however, was the Sachem's will.

The men of Plimoth, being obsessed with all manner of legal things, insisted Metacomet keep a will and testament in the event that he perished. As Sachem, he personally owned many things, including jewelry, wampum, hunting camps, and farmlands. Naturally, as one of the few who spoke and wrote English well enough to understand these things, Sassamon composed the will in English after Metacomet explained his wishes.

Although he tried to obscure his deviousness with legal terminology and mumbo-jumbo that Linto could scarcely understand, it was clear that in the event of his death, most of the Sachem's estate would fall into the hands of Sassamon himself. Linto's head was spinning. He read the document three times to ensure the strange language was not confusing him. He had no doubts. He had to tell Metacomet at once that his suspicions about Sassamon were correct.

Sassamon returned from Plimoth two days later. He was greeted by an emotionless Wampanoag council, which convened, as usual, at Metacomet's "throne," the mysterious and imposing formation of quartz rock. The Sachem brought the council to order with minimal fanfare.

"Sassamon, we have been having a great debate in your absence. Linto has been able to teach us much, but not enough. As you are so wise and learned, please help your people to understand."

Sassamon was alert and relaxed, as questions about the ways of the English were quite common. He reminisced about some previous ones. Why do the English warriors like to stand shoulder-to-shoulder "at attention" and remain perfectly still? How do they tolerate and promote the consumption of intoxicating beverages among the Indians but discourage it among themselves? If the ancient book tells them to "love their enemy," how does that affect their effectiveness in combat?

Metacomet was subdued as he continued. "Does the big, ancient book really teach the Christians that money is the root of all evil?"

"Yes, Sachem. That is in the second half, the newer part. Jesus, the gentle Son, denounced the love of worldly possessions because they separated people from Him."

Metacomet nodded his comprehension. "I think I understand. Doesn't the new part also talk about serving two masters?"

"Absolutely. Sachem, your learning and wisdom has become very impressive, indeed. In one of the four *gospels*, it was addressed." Sassamon enunciated the word as if Metacomet was a small child. "The gentle Son said a man cannot serve God and mammon. Mammon is a fancy English word for greedy love of money."

"Sassamon, I am learning so much about this English religion. And wasn't the gentle Son captured and murdered because he was betrayed by one of his closest advisors?"

Sassamon finally had an inkling that all was not well, and he hoped he was not perspiring. "Yes, Sachem. One of the most hated figures in history, Judas Iscariot, sold out his master for thirty pieces of silver." He knew the sweat was cascading down his face.

Metacomet stepped forward and set his powerful hand upon Sassamon's shoulder. "Wasn't there a kiss on the cheek as well?" Sassamon was quivering and unable to formulate a response.

"I am certain you understand, Sassamon, how well Linto reads and writes English now. I am certain you comprehend the magnitude of your betrayal. I am certain you understand how much you have stolen from me and the Wampanoag. I wonder what manner of peace and happiness it could have brought you."

He continued. "Sassamon, I know the Wampanoag and the Narragansett and the Nipmuc have a few thieves in their midst. I know the thieving ways of the English, and I do not think highly of the Dutch. It is the nature of this world, this obsession with money. Money generates a mental sickness, a fanaticism that befalls so many of us. But Sassamon..." He gripped his shoulder tighter. "Sassamon, look in my eyes and tell me you have not been reporting our thoughts and actions to Skunk Genitals." Tobias and Mentayyup were now standing, and Linto was certain Tobias was going to wrap his hands around Sassamon's throat. Sassamon, now quivering with remarkable intensity, said nothing.

The Sachem released his grip and continued. "Shall we hold a trial, Sassamon? The way the English do? Shall we put on fancy clothes and sit indoors and have English justice?"

Sassamon did the most rational thing he could do. He spun away and sprinted down the hill. He was too terrified to turn around and see if anyone was pursuing him. Tobias was choosing an appropriate weapon and was ready to begin the hunt.

"Let him run!" Metacomet restrained Tobias by his

arm, much to his horror. "Do not assault him. Let him run. He will scurry back to Skunk Genitals. For what does the big, ancient book say?" He thoughtfully cocked his head and paused.

"Ah yes. A dog will return to its own vomit."

CHAPTER FOURTEEN

PROVIDENCE

Three days? Certainly, no more than four?

Brewster was pensive as he embarked on his walk to the meeting house. He thought long and hard about not attending and incurring the wrath of Easton. How much punishment could he really incur for a drunken Bible recitation? Three days in prison? Brewster was under the impression Providence was relatively lenient and merciful about these things. What's more, he had strong doubts Easton was even serious, and he suspected the threat was made in jest.

These thoughts so occupied and distracted Brewster that he was stunned how quickly he arrived at his destination. He lingered casually outside the door. Easton was nowhere to be seen, but Brewster watched the faithful trickle in, each one more welcoming and friendly than the previous. He made a pretense that he was just standing outside to meet someone, but he felt increasingly ridiculous and stepped inside.

Brewster agonized over a striking revelation: He was feeling extraordinary shame and trepidation. Brewster could picture the stern, disapproving eyes of his Plimoth neighbors and forefathers bearing down upon him as he entered this house of heresy. But this was not the source of his surprise.

What did surprise him, however, was on the night he was spun through the tavern by his ankles, he never envisioned Elder William Brewster shaking his head in grim, grandfatherly disapproval. When he woke up one painful morning behind the tavern, he did not see Increase Mather's handsome face quietly condemning him. When he tried to ride Brownie while sitting backwards, and was thrown clear off, the image of Josiah Winslow was not there to judge him.

And yet when he closed his eyes at this moment, there

they were. Brewster imagined the entire gallery of Puritan teachers, parents, clergymen, government officials, and former congregation members staring at him with their furious teeth clenching, ready to unleash their righteous and Godly wrath at the unholy Quaker dissident. Oh yes, and one deceased spouse.

As he was grievously stung by that last thought, John Easton found him, and with a delighted smile, guided him into the meeting house. Brewster could only imagine the sacrilege that awaited him. Upon taking in his surroundings, he was immediately astonished.

He anticipated an orderly arrangement of rigid wooden pews aligned to face an authoritative altar where the minister could direct the proceedings. Instead he was greeted by a circle of chairs, and not a particularly well-arranged circle. Brewster had always prided himself on the way the Separatists and Puritans had stripped away the popish ostentation of worship that bedeviled the Anglican Church, but this congregation had exceeded even Middleborough's virtuous austerity. And then there was the silence.

Brewster took a seat next to Easton and waited for something to start. And waited. And waited. When would the minister arrive and when would worship begin? Evidently the minister was detained somewhere because the three dozen or so members of the congregation just sat there. In order to put the time to good use Brewster bowed his head and mentally recited the fortieth Psalm.

"I waited patiently for the Lord; and he inclined unto me, and heard my cry. He brought me up also out of a horrible pit, out ..."

And Brewster's reverie was interrupted. A young woman, probably no older than sixteen, began singing. With no permission asked or received, there was unannounced, spontaneous *singing*! He was almost relieved when it ended. He sat in silence for what must have been another ten minutes. This was lunacy. No wonder the Puritans reviled this heresy so passionately. And then, out of nowhere, a woman rose to speak. *Another woman*! Another woman, doing whatever she felt like doing *during a worship service*.

She spoke confidently and articulately. "Friends, hear my voice, for the light of the resurrected Christ is within me and it is within you. I have been earnestly praying, and I have been grieving for this land. For when friends extend their hands for the blessings of the Lord, they are instead given a bottle of liquor. When children are hungry and cry out, they receive the wicked blows of anger and wrath. When Indians clamor for justice, they are shown the barrel of a musket. And when the Lord's people cry out for freedom, they are shown the chains of human bondage. I pray the power of the Lord will crush and revile the evil of Satan and the slavery that pervades this land. I will dedicate myself, with the power of the Almighty, to fight the wickedness and oppression the governments of these colonies embrace. Amen."

If this woman removed her clothing and danced around a fire, Brewster would not have been more stunned than he already was. Here was a parishioner, *a woman,* who to the best of his knowledge had no formal training in the ministry, standing and speaking in church without permission, and denouncing the governments of the colonies? Brewster slouched quietly in his chair and waited for the door to be knocked down and the militia to burst in, so this appalling troublemaker could be carried away.

And so it went for more than an hour. Silence interrupted by spontaneous outbursts. Singing. Calls for mercy and justice. Exclamations of gratitude. No ministers, no sermon, no psalmody, no talk of sin and damnation. And Brewster felt so shocked and confused he could scarcely formulate his feelings.

After he led a group prayer, Deputy Governor Easton casually blessed and dismissed the congregation. With his hand on Brewster's shoulder, he warmly insisted he follow him home for tea and breakfast. Brewster was too dumbfounded by the proceedings to decline.

He was soon made comfortable in the Eastons' lovely home. The deputy governor introduced himself more formally, and soon Brewster and he were well acquainted.

John Easton had been born and baptized in the mother country, but sailed for the new world at age nine. He sailed with his father and brother, as his mother died shortly after the birth and death of a child. Brewster immediately felt a kinship.

They settled in Massachusetts Bay, but his father became devoted to religious dissidents such as Anne Hutchinson. His family were soon exiles, and Easton found himself in the colony of Rhode Island. This is where Easton devoted himself to the Quaker faith and public service.

His wife and children were lovely, and Easton introduced Mrs. Easton as Mehitable, which was certainly one of the most unique English names Brewster had ever heard, perhaps even on par with Increase. It was derived from the Old Testament and meant "God rejoices."

Brewster devoured his second cup of tea and was feeling at ease. "Were you really going to lock me up for reciting the kings of Israel if I didn't show up today?"

Easton threw his head back and laughed. "Lock you up? We should bestow a medal on you of some kind. I was in awe. Do you know the Kings of Judah, too?"

Brewster took the bait. "Rehoboam, Abijam, Asa, Jehoshaphat..."

Easton threw his head back again, and a warm, boisterous laugh filled the room. "Enough, enough Brewster. My, what a gift. Indeed." He suddenly turned serious.

"Israel, what happened in Plimoth?"

Brewster almost dropped his tea. The burning sense of shame returned, and he looked at his shoes. He finally composed himself. "Whatever happens in these matters?

They decide what is righteous and who is wicked. They are terrified of the ways of the Indians, and I guess I drew too close to them. Maybe I'm deluded, but I suspect somehow romantic jealousy played a role. Oh, and evidently they're not ready to forgive Mary Dyer."

Easton knew the circumstances of Brewster's disgrace but his eyes still grew wide at the mention of one of the great martyrs of his faith. "And what did you think of our gathering this morning?"

He chose his words carefully. "It was very nice and very interesting, I suppose. Not at all what I was expecting. When do you have the worship service?"

"That was the service, Reverend Brewster." Once again, Brewster was too stunned to speak. "Reverend Brewster, I know you Puritans and Separatists pride yourselves on eliminating all of the trappings of worship. All of the robes, incense, cathedrals, and hierarchy that ultimately separates the Christian from God. We like to think we've exceeded the Puritans in our zeal for simplifying and purifying."

"Who is the minister? When do you read from scripture? How does the congregation learn?" Brewster could have asked fifty successive questions.

"Israel…and I will not call you *Izzy*…our faith teaches the light of Christ is within each and every one of us. If we meditate in silence and block out the endless distractions of the world, the Lord will commune with each and every one of us, and we will express that as we are individually inspired. Let me turn things around and you can enlighten me. Tell me about predestination."

After a three-year exile, Brewster leapt at the chance to discuss Calvinist philosophy. "The world and mankind are fundamentally sinful and wicked. The Lord, in his infinite mercy, chose to extend His holy salvation to a very limited population. Their salvation was preordained from the beginning of time. These chosen, or *elect*, are assured of their salvation, and consequently lead a life that is pleasing to God, for they can live no other life. It is God's grace and mercy that renders them saved, however, and not a life of deeds or works. Surely you know and understand this."

"Oh, I am well aware of all of it. The question is, Reverend Israel Brewster, *do you believe it?* Do you believe this is how the divine creator ordered the world?" Brewster sat in uncomfortable silence, glaring at his empty tea cup.

"Israel, you don't have to answer that, and you don't have to come to any more worship among the Friends if you are not inclined. I don't wish to make you uncomfortable. But you do have to promise me one thing."

Brewster closed his eyes and waited for the demand. Would he have to resume his role as a clergyman? Would he promise to quit drinking? Perhaps Easton would demand Brewster return to Plimoth to face his accusers, the way so many martyrs did, instead of slinking away like a coward. He took a deep breath.

"Israel Brewster, you have to promise me you will not let your salvation, your inner goodness, and the light of the resurrected Christ that dwells within you be controlled, defined, or extinguished by anything the government of Plimoth or Massachusetts Bay ever does or says."

And in exchange for a third cup of tea, the Reverend Israel Brewster, the disgraced and exiled minister, the grandson of the noble Elder William Brewster, the barrel-maker, the widower, and the de facto owner of an insubordinate, flatulent horse, made that promise.

And his world suddenly felt very different.

CHAPTER FIFTEEN

MIDDLEBOROUGH

Joshua Farwell was being indecisive. Frankly, it was all for the best as he was reveling in the solitude. His home in Middleborough was joyous and noisy. His twin boys were now three years old, and Mary felt certain they were going to be blessed for a third time. They laughed, they hugged, and they thanked the Lord for their marriage.

He had followed the Nemasket River and had ventured more than two miles south of his home, all the way to Assawompset Pond. It was certainly a magnificent pond, more than a mile across in any direction. He was finding some magnificent trees as well, for his work as a cooper always demanded a bounty of workable lumber of excellent quality. Frequently, he had to deviate far from the beaten path in order to find what he was looking for.

On that particular day, Joshua had plenty of time to quietly think and meditate, and he put it to good use. He was wondering if he would be a good father and provider, and the thought of another child filled him with joy and anxiety. He knew that somehow, no matter the difficulties, the Lord would provide.

He wished he had a source of wise counsel during these times of self-doubt. Reverend Phelps and his wife Alice were certainly nice people, but the reverend always exuded an aura of cold smugness, and Joshua never saw fit to confide in him.

He tried not to think about it too much over these last few years, but he knew he missed Reverend Brewster terribly. His sermons were rousing and insightful, and his counsel was patient and wise. Joshua tried to remember a time when he saw Israel Brewster idle or at rest, and he could not. The

Reverend Phelps never seemed to help raise the new homes or prepare the fields for crops. He seemed to spend most of his time back in Plimoth. Joshua knew he owed Brewster a tremendous debt, and he was wrought with guilt over the small but discernible role he played in his downfall. Life was very difficult sometimes.

Joshua was evaluating a marvelous sycamore tree, and contemplated how much wood he was prepared to drag the two miles home. He had quite a few tools to procure the lumber and a rugged sled to drag behind him. He needed to make up his mind quickly, because late January was no time for a New England man to be dawdling in the woods by himself. He wasn't even sure Mary knew where to find him.

He took four steps backward to better survey the tree, and he oafishly tripped. Rising to his feet, and thankful no one was around to mock his awkwardness, he realized he had tripped over a man's hat. It was a slightly odd circumstance, but certainly the hapless and hatless soul was not the first to see his head covering fall victim to the vicious New England wind.

As he picked the hat up and inspected it, he congratulated himself on how witty a phrase "hapless and hatless" was. He must remember to tell Mary. Then from the corner of his eye, on the edge of the pond, he saw an odder sight. Someone had left a good portion of fishing gear on the bank.

Joshua became increasingly anxious and suspected he may not be alone. What manner of catastrophe would compel a man to abandon his hat and all of this gear? He yelled as loudly as he could, but was answered by the cold, frosty stillness of a lonely January day. He peered across the icy pond and turned around to look in every direction. He cupped his frigid hands to his mouth and yelled again. He even looked up at the sky. Then he gazed into the frozen pond and fell backwards with fright.

He quickly stood and composed himself, and he verified the unbearable sight was not a hallucination. There was a man entombed under the ice.

Joshua paused to collect his wits. He was certain the man was deceased, for how could he not be, but inexplicably Joshua felt a sense of fantastic urgency. He knew his actions would require careful consideration, and he surveyed the scene.

The ice apparently seemed strong enough to support his weight, but he knew the extraction process would be daunting. If he did not exhibit extreme care, he could easily be sharing the unfortunate stranger's fate.

He stepped back from the pond. The prudent thing to do would be to resign the stranger to his eternal rest and head back to town for assistance. As a father of two, potentially three children, it was pointless to risk his own welfare. Clearly the stranger was dead. Yet for some unknown reason he was compelled to extricate the tragic soul as quickly as possible. He uttered a brief prayer for strength and guidance, and he went to work.

Joshua wondered if it was divine intervention that he was so well equipped with hand tools. Kneeling on the ice, he was able to delicately crack and open the frozen tomb utilizing mallets, awls and handsaws, and he quickly made valuable progress. He still felt secure on his portion of the ice, and soon he had a realistic opportunity to remove the victim. Grabbing him from under his arms, he was able to fall backwards and then slide on his backside while pulling him along, simultaneously propelling himself as the bottom of his boots pushed against the ice. The stranger was free.

There would be no miracle at Assawompset Pond on the 29th day of January in the year 1675. The stranger was clearly deceased, and Joshua quickly noticed he was an Indian. He assumed he had fallen in the water while fishing. Perhaps he was intoxicated. Joshua's hands and arms were horrifically cold, and he wrestled with the notion of remaining in place and building a fire. He thought the better of it and was soon running the two miles to Middleborough with his sled in tow. It had been an eventful trip.

In the future, Joshua Farwell would tell his grandchildren about the day he discovered the body entombed in the ice. And his most vivid recollection would not be how terrified he was when he saw it, or how cautious he was when extracting it, or how witty "hatless and hapless" was. His most vivid recollection would be how quickly he navigated the two miles home to Middleborough with a corpse in tow. He felt as if he was divinely guided, for he suffered no frostbite or any other malady.

Joshua would also tell his grandchildren that nothing creates a commotion quite like racing into town while towing a dead, frozen Indian. Within minutes all of Middleborough was abuzz and leering at the body. Isaac Reddington, woken from his mid-afternoon slumber, briefly examined the body and made a shocking announcement. The victim's neck was clearly broken, and marks of strangulation were evident. Joshua felt foolish for not having noticed, but considering the situation, he certainly had nothing to apologize for. The evidence was initially difficult to notice, but after the body had a chance to warm, the tell-tale signs became more evident.

Just when the little hamlet of Middleborough reached the conclusion that the situation could not get any more exciting, Alice Phelps gazed at the poor man at eternal rest, and broke into tears.

"It's John, the praying Indian. The smart one from the missionary trips." Her voice quivered. "It's John Sassamon."

CHAPTER SIXTEEN

MONTAUP

Metacomet was not surprised. Frankly, it was just like Skunk Genitals Winslow to do something like this.

Approximately five sunsets after Sassamon's lifeless body was pulled from the pond, the Sachem of the Wampanoag received the news. It all made sense now. The English, with their deceitful spies everywhere, would have learned the Wampanoag were privy to Sassamon's vile deceit. Sassamon would have been no longer useful to Plimoth, but they would have had reason to fear him, too. Once Sassamon was exposed, they thought, he would be vulnerable to physical torture, and would reveal the secrets of the English spy network. Or perhaps, they thought Sassamon would make a pathetic effort to salvage his ill-gotten fortune, and would offer to secretly turn on the English.

No matter which scenario Metacomet envisioned, it was clear to him an exposed Sassamon was an unacceptable liability to the English, and they had to murder him. Frankly, the frozen pond and the fishing gear struck him as a pathetic attempt at subterfuge, but no matter. Sassamon received his just rewards, and the Wampanoag were much better for it. The Sachem hoped that in some small way, his elimination would help maintain the fragile peace.

Approximately one moon later, however, Metacomet realized that no matter what despicable treachery he thought the English were capable of, they always found a way to exceed his expectations. For on that day, the Sachem received word that while on a hunting trip, Tobias, his son Wampapaquan, and young Mattashunnamo were seized by the English. The irony of being seized during a hunting trip sickened him, and Metacomet cursed Skunk Genitals for his cowardly inability to march to Montaup and present his evidence. Even if the trio did kill Sassamon, which they certainly did not, what right did the English have to oversee this affair? Sassamon was not an Englishman.

The Sachem subsequently learned that the three accused Wampanoag would remain incarcerated until they would stand trial in the summer. The English and their courts. The English and their justice. What a farce. Metacomet knew they would, as usual, bring six Christian Indians to sit with the jury, to demonstrate how fair and unbiased they were. Unbiased, indeed. Metacomet wished the men of Plimoth would just be men and let Tobias fight five of them to the death. That would resolve this matter, and quickly.

The situation was desperate, and Metacomet knew what he had to do. He had to go see Linto.

Linto looked like he had not slept in ten sunsets. He was thinner than ever and fatherhood was dimming his radiant smile. "My Sachem. Is there trouble?"

"Linto, you have heard the news. Skunk Genitals Winslow has arrested them and thrown them in prison. While they were hunting. *Hunting, Linto! Hunting!*"

"Yes, I am aware and it is disgraceful. The men of Plimoth are capable of anything. Sassamon's blood is probably on their hands, but they will condemn Tobias."

"They say they will stand trial before the summer solstice. But it is all a big show they like to put on. They will be convicted and they will be executed. And then..." Linto knew where this was going.

"Linto, I do not believe I can restrain the rage of the young warriors anymore. I know many think of me as a weak English puppet since I yielded to Plimoth three summers ago. However, I am not certain I want to restrain them anymore. If the English take Tobias and the others from me..." The Sachem turned away. "We have surrendered enough, Linto. We have surrendered for too long."

And once again Linto, the holy, miraculous Linto, prayed for an answer. Something had to be done, and quickly. The thought of total warfare throughout the colony was unbearable. He could not permit Wawetseka and their two young children to experience a life of incessant warfare, starvation, and inevitable death at the hands of the English.

So Linto spoke. In retrospect, it was as if the words just flowed from his mouth with no thought whatsoever. For if he had taken the time to consider his words, it was doubtful he would have said what he said.

"Sachem, let me stand for Tobias."

Metacomet was perplexed. "Stand for him?"

"Isn't that the way the English settle these things? Don't the accused get to have a man argue for them? I think that is how many of the fancy men in Boston make their money. I will be his counselor."

"I should stand for him."

"Sachem, you are the bravest and wisest among us, but their bizarre way of speaking is still a mystery to you. I can speak to the men at the Plimoth Court. I can tell them Tobias and the two are innocent. I can explain it to them."

Metacomet was deep in thought. He slowly paced, and Linto thought he might walk away without a word. Finally, he spoke. "We will rely on you once again, Linto. You have been sent to the Wampanoag for a reason and I know your work is not done yet. Speak for Tobias and the others. Speak the truth, and do not tolerate falsehood. If Plimoth can be made to see the errors of their way, and the three are returned to us, there may yet be hope."

He held Linto by the shoulders and continued. "You are a blessing upon us, Linto. Do not forget that. I will tell the others of your plan. I will tell them the wonderful news." The Sachem quickly turned and was gone. And Linto remained sitting, staring at the ground with his head hung low.

For Linto had absolutely no idea what he would say

and do at Plimoth General Court.

CHAPTER SEVENTEEN

PLIMOTH

Linto felt very warm in his fancy English shirt. He wanted to look presentable so he wore leggings and moccasins, forced his hair back with fish oil, and wore a big black shirt with a big white collar. Fortunately, he was not wearing one of the enormous puffy collars so many of the Plimoth men were wearing. They looked like they were trapped. Although the hour was early, the month was June and the courtroom was stifling.

Linto presented himself to the court three weeks ago, and respectfully requested that he be permitted to serve as counselor to the accused. Since he had been the only volunteer for the position, he was accepted with no squabble. Linto was probably a familiar face because during the preceding weeks, he spent as much time as he could reading their books and watching the Plimoth Court settle criminal matters.

His status as counselor also afforded him the opportunity to see the defendants during their incarceration. The two young men had difficulty containing their fear, but Tobias, as expected, appeared resentful and brave. They had been properly fed but the confinement was increasingly unbearable, especially during the long days of summer.

And now their day of judgement had arrived. Linto rose when he was directed to, and he gazed with wonder upon the Great Seal of Plimoth. Why were there four people? Were they supposed to be Indians? Why were they each kneeling and holding an enormous apple? Or was that supposed to be a heart? Why were their hearts not in their chests? Linto silently cursed himself for not investigating this matter earlier.

When he was seated, he scanned the men of the jury.

The jury was enormous, since, in an Indian matter such as this, in addition to the regular jury, there were six Indians. Of course, as far as Linto was aware, they were all Christian. Still, it was a pleasing attempt to create an aura of objectivity.

After the initial fanfare, the charges were read aloud. The three defendants stood expressionless as they listened.

"At a place called Assawompset Pond, the defendants willfully and of set purpose and of malice aforethought, and by force and arms, did murder John Sassamon, another Indian, by laying violent hands on him, and striking him, or twisting his neck until he was dead, and to hide and conceal this said murder, at the time and place aforesaid, did cast his dead body through a hole in the ice into said pond."

Linto listened to the words carefully. Aforesaid. A-fore-said. He often wondered why it seemed the men of Plimoth were speaking a language other than English.

"And how do these three men plead before this lawful and holy court?"

The three defendants remained silent and morose as if they would not even acknowledge and dignify the proceedings.

Linto realized it was time to speak. "With all due respect to the King of England, Plimoth Colony, and this lawful court. I am Linto of the Wampanoag, and I am counselor to the accused. These men are innocent, and that is how they plead."

Instead of one judge, the proceedings were overseen by a council of five stern Plimoth men. One of them, with a screechy, irritating voice, loudly replied, "are these Indians not capable of speaking?" His bulbous eyes bore down upon the defendants.

Linto nodded at Tobias and he finally stepped forward. His English skills had improved during his incarceration. "We are innocent. We did not murder Sassamon." Linto was uncertain if that satisfied the seemingly insatiable need for formality and fanfare among the English, but it seemed to suffice.

"Very well. The prosecution may proceed." The gentleman who would direct the prosecution against Tobias, his son Wampapaquan, and Mattashunnamo was a short, ruddy man with a rotund nose. Any gifts he lacked in personal appearance were almost balanced by his voice, a beautiful and elegant baritone that resonated through the room, almost creating the impression the heavens had opened and the creator was speaking. His name was Bartholomew Fletcher, and he anticipated an easy day of serving justice in Plimoth Colony.

The first witness was Doctor Samuel Fuller. Doctor Fuller seemed to be quite aged, and as Linto scoured his memory, he was increasingly certain this must be the same man who provided the "working physic" to Wamsutta. Doctor Fuller calmly and methodically testified that, in accordance with tradition, John Sassamon's corpse was recovered, and the primary defendant was forced to confront it. Allegedly, as Tobias approached Sassamon's corpse, it began to bleed. This was a certain testament to Tobias' guilt.

Linto listened and was horrified. Tobias had told him of the ordeal, and Linto could scarcely believe it. Sassamon's corpse would have been dead and buried for months, but it was disinterred for this ghastly spectacle. Linto hoped and assumed he would be able to ask Doctor Fuller about all of this, and he was given his opportunity. Linto mentally pledged to remain calm, respectful, and polite.

"Good morning, Doctor. Thank you for permitting me some questions." Doctor Fuller shifted uncomfortably in his chair. Educated, articulate Indians often seemed unsettling to him.

"Now, doctor, please tell us who was present when this test was conducted." The doctor paused and looked up to the council, still uncertain if he was required to answer questions from this interloper. He inferred from their silence that he was.

"I was there. The man who strangled John Sassamon to death was there. Two lawful constables of Plimoth Colony were there."

Linto considered the doctor's words. "Doctor, my understanding of English law is that it is improper to refer to the accused in such a negative manner. They may very well be proven innocent today." Doctor Fuller once again looked at the council for guidance. The screechy man seemed to be rolling his eyes. Doctor Fuller gave no reply.

"Tell me Doctor, would it have been appropriate to have another witness at the proceeding? Someone who could have corroborated this alleged bleeding?"

Doctor Fuller was not pleased. "I do not know the meaning of your words. I was there and two sworn constables were there. We all saw the bleeding. Do you dare to imply we are not truthful?"

Linto carefully chose his words. "Of course not, sir. I am merely trying to understand and follow all of the traditions of English law. I was under the impression that during such a critical examination, an individual not associated with the prosecution might also be present. Forgive me. Doctor, what happened when the constables approached the body?"

"I'm sorry?"

"Certainly, in the name of science, a man not accused of the crime also approached the body, in order to objectively assess the results and ensure the victim did not bleed?"

"No, this examination does not require such excess. For surely it is known, that when a murderer approaches the corpse of his victim, the victim will bleed."

"Does the Bible teach us this?"

There was an immediate thrall of whispers and muttering when this remarkably articulate Indian, previously unknown to them, mentioned the Bible. The presiding officials had to demand silence.

Linto continued. "For I know that in the book of Leviticus, Moses spoke *the life of the flesh is in the blood.* I also know the laws the Lord set forth for females..." Linto was referencing the King James Bible in the courtroom by this point. *"And if a woman have an issue, and her issue in her flesh be blood, she shall be put apart seven days; and whosoever toucheth her shall be unclean until the evening.* So there are clearly laws about blood regarding females and their cycles and childbirths. And I believe it is the book of Psalms...yes...here it is. *Deliver me from bloodguiltiness, O God, thou God of my salvation: and my tongue shall sing aloud of thy righteousness.* And, Doctor Fuller, let us hear the words of the prophet Jeremiah. *But know ye for certain, that if ye put me to death, ye shall surely bring innocent blood upon yourselves, and upon this city, and upon the inhabitants thereof: for of a truth the LORD hath sent me unto you to speak all these words in your ears."*

The whispers were rising to a steady chorus of disbelief. Linto, in his quest to master English, had developed an astounding knowledge of the Bible, and after Tobias recounted the blood ritual, Linto prepared obsessively. "Doctor, as far as I can tell, there are hundreds of references to *blood* in holy scripture. In which chapter is this test of blood guilt mentioned?"

The doctor was growing irritated. "I do not know."

"It is, of course, divinely sanctioned and in the Bible, is it not? For certainly, there are laws and guidance in the Bible pertaining to blood and murder. I cannot, however, seem to find it. Tell me, doctor, what is the origin of this mysterious test for guilt?"

"It is tradition. Every doctor and clergyman is aware of it."

"But where did it come from? I am but a humble Wampanoag and wish to learn."

The presiding officials felt the urge to end this line of inquiry several minutes ago, but by now they had no doubt.

"Mister Linto, we have heard enough on this topic. There is historic legal precedent for Doctor Fuller's test, and we will not tolerate any further insinuations or heresy."

Linto had made his point and knew when it was time to quit. He hoped the jury would be mentally doubting the value of Doctor Fuller's testimony. "Thank you, sir. I am complete and I am most grateful to Doctor Fuller for his time."

Linto suspected Doctor Fuller would be a prelude to the main event and he was absolutely correct. For at that point, Bartholomew Fletcher introduced the court to the foundation of the case. This was the witness who would alleviate any doubt in a jury's mind, and would ensure the heathen murderers were lawfully punished. This was an Indian whose brave, truthful testimony would ensure justice. In his mellifluous baritone, Bartholomew Fletcher called forth Mister Patuckson.

Secrets were a precious commodity in Plimoth Colony, and everyone with a casual interest in the case was aware that shortly after Sassamon's corpse was discovered, it was Patuckson who went to the Plimoth authorities to identify his murderers.

Fletcher quickly and decisively got to the heart of the matter. Patuckson was covertly positioned on a hilltop above the pond and could see everything. He saw them assault the defenseless John Sassamon. He saw Tobias strangle him and break his neck. He saw them plant fishing gear at his side. And he saw them entomb Sassamon under the ice. Finally, Patuckson testified to his own devout Christianity, and the frequent blasphemy from the trio of pagans. Fletcher was complete in mere moments, and the courtroom was on edge. Linto wondered if there were men outside preparing the gallows.

Linto was grateful he was still permitted to speak after badgering Doctor Fuller. He attempted to be calm and methodical. But conversely, he was concerned that the presiding officials would silence him again the moment things became uncomfortable. He would have to strike quickly.

"Patuckson, how much money do you owe Tobias due to gambling debts?"

If the courtroom was previously on edge, it now devolved into open chaos as audience and jury members stood, yelled, laughed their approval or screamed their outrage. The presiding officials were demanding order and then turned their righteous wrath upon Linto.

"Mister Linto. Mister Patuckson clearly saw the murder transpire. Any activities or deeds that are external to the murder are ancillary, irrelevant, and not to be discussed in this court. May I remind you that you are privileged to be addressing us today, and that privilege can be revoked instantly."

Linto, once again, exhibited his practiced humility. "Forgive me sir, for I have much to learn." Mentally, Linto was delighted. They can reprimand and belittle him all they like, but the jury would not be able to forget his words.

Linto pressed ahead with his questioning. "Mister Patuckson, could you please tell this court more about this hillside you were positioned upon?"

Patuckson seemed instantly flustered and did not seem to have an answer. Almost inadvertently, he blurted out, "it was hilly?"

The court burst with uproarious laughter as the overbearing Indian got his comeuppance. Linto smiled and remained composed. "I meant, can you tell us which hill it was? Were you north of the pond? South of the pond? Were there trees on the hill?"

Patuckson went through the pretense of thinking. After a long pause, he uttered, "no, I am sorry, I cannot recall." Linto expected as much. Patuckson's mastery of English was as impressive as Linto's, and he would be a difficult adversary.

"Perhaps you can tell us why you were there?"

"Excuse me?"

"It was indeed fortuitous that you were on a hilltop overlooking the pond when the murders took place. Why were you there?"

Patuckson's cool composure finally started to develop cracks. He appeared visibly nervous and looked to Fletcher for guidance. "I…I saw them pushing and assaulting John Sassamon and dragging him away and knew I should pursue them…from a safe distance."

"I see. And where did the incident begin? Where did you witness the assault take place?"

"It was…east of the pond. Definitely east, about one mile." As a praying Indian, Patuckson was familiar with the English units of measure.

Linto seemed delighted. "I see. And why were you one mile east of Assawompset Pond at that particular time?" Patuckson was clearly unraveling, and his eyes darted around the court in hopes of intervention.

Fletcher rose. "Mister Linto has badgered this Christian witness enough. He has accurately testified to his location and Mister Linto needs to refrain from further hostility. Whether Mister Patuckson was hunting, or travelling home, or looking for good fishing is completely irrelevant." The presiding officials, unsurprisingly, agreed.

"Forgive me, Mister Patuckson. Now, you said the incident began one mile east of the pond, correct?"

Patuckson felt the need to reinforce his statement. "Yes, absolutely."

"So clearly you are familiar with Assawompset Pond and how it is situated?"

"Certainly."

"Then please let the court know. Where was the body entombed?"

"It was under the ice. You should pay attention,

Linto." Chuckles and guffaws ensued.

Linto patiently waited for the mirthful clamor to subside. "No, I mean, where in relation to the pond? Was it near the north bank, or the south? Perhaps the pond was so frozen it was in the center? Perhaps it was the east bank, near your position?"

Patuckson now glared frantically at Fletcher, who knew it was time to take action. He rose. "Gentlemen, I believe it is clear…" There was no need for him to rise as he was instantly interrupted by the screechy official.

"Mister Linto, we have heard quite enough of your desperate attempts to cause confusion and uncertainty in this Christian witness. You may take your seat. Mister Patuckson, please accept our apologies." Linto struggled not to smirk.

Surprisingly, Fletcher had no more witnesses and was summarizing the heinous actions inflicted on the poor, suffering John Sassamon. He implored the jury to do their duty to the laws of Plimoth Colony and the holy scripture.

Linto, perhaps presumptuously, assumed he would get the opportunity to speak one last time and solemnly rose.

"Sir, forgive me, but I am confused. When is Mister Fletcher going to finish his proceeding?"

"Mister Linto, he has successfully completed his prosecution and has provided a summation. Weren't you already advised to pay closer attention?" The chuckling was much more subdued this time.

"Forgive me, yet again. I was merely confused because I was awaiting the second witness. I believe, according to the laws of the colony, that a trial, especially a murder trial, requires two witnesses."

"Mister Linto, I have been very patient with you. Did you not personally question the two witnesses the prosecution presented?"

Linto stared at the floor. "I did do that, yes sir. But my understanding was that, absent a confession of the accused, two direct witnesses are required for an accusation of murder. And Doctor Fuller, though very learned, was not a direct witness to the act." Once again, the room was in an uproar, for they knew this disagreeable Indian was absolutely correct. If the court was unable to find a second direct witness, they were required to address the deficiency.

"Mister Linto, although your learning is impressive, your lack of understanding clearly is an irritant. During special circumstances, at the court's discretion, if the crime is hideous enough and threatens the security of this colony, one direct witness will be adequate. And we shall not hear another word from you Mister Linto."

The official leaned back in his chair, savoring the shame he caused Linto, and congratulating himself on his timely action. He thought how thankful he was that Governor Prence had finally met his eternal reward. Prence would have burdened and hindered the court with all manner of legalisms about the lack of two direct witnesses. Indian affairs were so much more efficient now that Winslow was governor.

Linto looked crestfallen and defeated as he hung his head. "Yes, sir." But inside his mind he was dancing and celebrating, for he had done it. He cast a knowing glance at Tobias. Weeks and months of reading tedious English law books and watching appallingly dull legal proceedings had borne fruit.

No matter how much the court tried to silence and ridicule him, the jury had heard everything. The jury knew how archaic and ridiculous Fuller's blood ritual was. The jury knew Patuckson was catastrophically indebted to Tobias. They could clearly see Patuckson was nowhere near the pond that day and was not only lying, but doing a terrible job of it. And finally, they knew one direct witness was not enough for the accused to be punished. A guilty sentence would be a mockery of all the books, laws, and scripture the English held so dear.

Somehow, he had done it. Linto, the child of destiny. He was delivered into the hands of the Wampanoag for a sacred purpose. Was this it, or would there be more triumphs to come? Linto had scarcely finished his mental celebration, when ten minutes later the jury reconvened.

And at that moment, Linto received the only lesson in English justice that he would ever truly need.

CHAPTER EIGHTEEN

PLIMOTH

During all the years Linto had studied the English language, he had come to be mystified and enthralled by all the nuances and intricacies. The double meanings, the bizarre spellings, the metaphors, and the subtleties always intrigued him.

At the moment, he was considering the word "numb." When he first learned the word, it sounded delightfully simple, and he repeated it over and over like a child: "Numb numb numb." Why on earth was there a letter "B" at the end? Linto tried to enunciate the sound. "Num...Bah! Num...BEE!" It made him feel ridiculous.

He was also intrigued by the word due to its various contexts. He understood its fundamental meaning described the inability to move or feel. It was a lack of sensation, possibly due to cold or an injury. By extension, it also evoked the sensation of being so overwhelmed by a traumatic event, that the "numb" person was unable to respond to any external stimuli. He now understood that particular experience completely.

When the jury came back and announced Tobias, Wampapaquan, and Mattashunnamo were guilty as charged, and the screechy Englishman declared they would be hung by their necks at dawn, Linto was rendered numb. He was standing, but he could feel no sensation in his hands or feet. He was unable to speak, and in hindsight he was almost certain he could not see or hear for approximately ten seconds. When he did hear, he was overwhelmed by an odd, constant, ringing sensation.

And at that moment Linto learned everything he needed to know about the Plimoth legal system and English justice. The English were civilized, the Wampanoag were not.

They were the chosen elect of God, and Linto's people were not. Consequently, truth was a disposable, malleable entity to be contorted and disposed of whenever and however the English required.

Wampapaquan and Mattashunnamo had begun gently sobbing, and Linto had no doubt Tobias would, if he was not restrained by irons, begin murdering his enemies, starting with Patuckson. Linto did not know what to do.

He contemplated returning to Montaup to convey the tragic news and beg the Sachem's forgiveness, but he knew there were other Wampanoag in the chambers who were already on their way. Metacomet had prudently kept his distance from the proceedings, fearing he would be a distraction, and fearing the English would find a legalism to seize and incarcerate him as well. Linto, however, more than anything else, wished to be with the accused on that night.

As their legal counsel, after much pleading and demanding, he was permitted to spend the night with them in their prison cell. On some level Linto wondered if the English sense of justice was so perverted that they might just hang him too, since he would already be in a prison cell and he publicly annoyed them. So be it. Linto felt so broken he was prepared for any travesty that could befall him.

Before joining them in the cell Linto spent time begging and cajoling anyone in the vicinity in order to procure rations for the condemned. Some semblance of Christian charity was finally made manifest, as many of the townswomen provided bread, cheese, apples, and meat pies.

Linto wondered if the trio would live to see Metacomet rushing to Plimoth with a hundred warriors. He knew that was just a fantasy as the town was fortified like no other, and he was uncertain how many warriors the Sachem could even assemble. Metacomet would be devastated. How could Linto possibly face him?

Linto cursed his own idiocy. His own naive, pathetic,

inflated view of "Linto the chosen one" had led him to this disaster. He had given these three men false hope, and then he failed dismally. He felt ashamed.

He finally had the courage to face Tobias. "Forgive me, my brother, because I have failed you. I thought I was wise enough and cunning enough to foil the English wickedness, but I was wrong. Forgive me."

"Linto, I am the one begging forgiveness, because I never saw you until today. I resented you for your entire life. I scowled at you and ignored you. I despised the special treatment you received from the Sachems and the elders. But now I see. You are brilliant, and you are special. Who among our people could have stood up in an English courtroom and exposed their folly for all to see?

"I know my execution was preordained, Linto. There could be twenty Wampanoag who saw me days from that pond, but if one praying Indian says I was there…that is enough. No one could have stopped this."

Wampapaquan had been huddled in the corner, sobbing once again. Linto was amazed how, once again, he seemed so very young to him. Losing Tobias was inconceivable, but the thought of the two young men being extinguished in the prime of their lives filled Linto with rage. He spoke freely.

"There will be war. There is no stopping it now."

Tobias merely nodded. "Did you think you would ever be a warrior, Linto? Will you carry a musket?"

Linto's eyes went wide at the prospect. For all the incessant talk of war these last few years, he never contemplated his role. As a turtle, he would be expected to fulfill a duty similar to an English chaplain, but with more medical expertise. He could not conceive being useful in that function. He also suspected Metacomet would not permit him to be in harm's way.

"I don't know, Tobias. I really don't."

Tobias smiled and placed his hand on Linto's knee in a fatherly gesture. "I know you are brave, Linto. Do not ever doubt yourself." There was a pause as Tobias removed his hand and stared into Linto's eyes. "Promise me something, Linto."

Linto was still, and he dreaded what might come next.

"Grant a dying man his wish, Linto, and promise me something. Promise me you will never let Metacomet humiliate himself before the English again."

The words made Linto panic. He had so many reasons to deny Tobias. He did not know what the future would bring. He despised the thought of war and could not envision how the English could be defeated. He didn't even know if he would have any influence whatsoever with Metacomet after his crushing defeat today. But in less than twelve hours, Tobias would be hung by his neck until he was dead.

Linto nodded. "Yes, yes. I promise, Tobias. I promise."

Linto fought the urge to ask the question he had been dying to ask all these weeks. *Did Tobias do it?* Linto knew it was a strong possibility, perhaps even a probability. But he would never expose these three condemned men to that indignity on their final night.

They spent the remainder of the evening singing songs and praying. Tobias told hunting stories and wished he had some rum. Linto had genuinely tried but was unable to procure any. Tobias spent the majority of the night comforting the young men, especially his son. They were told to set aside their fears and be prepared to meet their eternal reward as Wampanoag warriors and members of the wolf clan.

Linto was ashamed that after weeks and months of crying babies and English legal books, the exhaustion and the darkness of the cell finally overtook him, and he fell asleep. Tobias did not wake him. Soon there were tiny rays of sunlight piercing his eyes. It was dawn. As the constables came for the condemned, Linto stood mute.

Tobias leaned over and spoke. "I am blessed I will never have to spend another moment in this dark cell, and soon, I will never have to see another Englishman. Tell Metacomet I died with honor and dignity. Thank you for all you have done, and remember your promise, Linto."

The men were violently whisked away to the site of their execution. Soldiers marched and drummers drummed. Their convictions were read aloud, and Linto noticed the proceeding had attracted quite an audience.

The three were escorted up the stairs to the gallows, accompanied by a minister whom they ignored as he chanted comforting verses. They were offered the opportunity to say their final words. Just as Linto expected, Tobias screamed a profane tirade to let the assembly know he was a warrior, he was not afraid of them, and soon the land of his ancestors would be free of the English disease. Despite Tobias' admonishments, Wampapaquan and Mattashunnamo were sobbing and had no final words. The hoods were placed over their heads and the English drummers made the "bbrrrrrr" sound with their drumsticks.

And Linto could do nothing. He had prayed so much during the last twelve hours. He prayed so intensely for a miracle, but nothing had happened. He prayed that somehow his mere presence as the chosen one among his people would somehow be the impetus for a divine intervention. But now the nooses were around their necks and there would be no miracle.

Linto diverted his eyes as the supports were kicked away, and the men swung. He heard the audience cry out and the women swoon. He refocused his eyes on the platform, expecting to see three lifeless, swinging corpses.

And then there was a miracle.

One of the three men had fallen to the platform and

was writhing and desperately kicking. Linto was confident it was Wampapaquan but he could not be certain. The prisoner was screaming in terror, and with a nod from the constable, an attendant removed his hood. It was Wampapaquan, and he was lying beside the broken rope that was tied around his neck.

A broken rope! Surely this was some form of divine intervention. This was the spirit world, letting the material world know in no uncertain terms this man was wrongfully convicted. Linto's spiritual epiphany was shattered as Wampapaquan, clearly tainted by a puddle of his own urine, desperately cried out in mangled English.

"I tell you everything! Everything! Do not hang me again! It was Father! Tobias! Father killed him and we watched! No choice, Metacomet order him do killing! I kill nobody! Let me live, tell you everything! Metacomet and Father! Metacomet and Father!"

The assembled citizens were astonished, and the minister implored the Almighty for guidance. Young Wampapaquan had tasted a split-second of violent death, and he would do anything to not experience it again. The constables and attendants were awkward and paralyzed, with no one having a clue what to do next. The rope was examined, and they were stunned such a healthy rope could be shredded by such a skinny victim. It was as if they had completely forgotten about the two successful executions, and the condemned men were left dangling without a thought. Linto knew what he had to do.

"A divine intervention! Heaven has spoken!" He yelled as loudly as possible, and one or two bystanders gasped. "Is there not an English tradition, NAY, is it not English LAW that if a condemned man is hung and the rope breaks, and the man lives, that man is NOT to be hung again? For certainly, I say, the English God has cast his disapproval on this execution! There cannot be another hanging!"

The Plimoth authorities huddled and feverishly conferred. None of them had experienced anything like this. Was the Indian right? Was this a sign of disapproval from the Almighty? How could they hang him again and risk the consequences?

But what was that talk about Metacomet? Was it the raving lunacy of a dying man? Or could the authorities ascertain that Metacomet ordered this assassination, and would he have to be held accountable?

The authorities concluded that the only logical course of action would be to tread carefully. They would hold the prisoner in his cell and confer with church elders about the significance of this event. The prisoner would be questioned extensively about Metacomet.

Linto was dismissed. He inquired about the remains of the condemned and was informed that, regarding the Indians, there was no precedent to release the bodies of convicted murderers back to their loved ones and the remains would be appropriately disposed of.

The council would earnestly confer about the Wampapaquan situation, especially regarding his comments about Metacomet. The council would send a messenger to Montaup in three days with their decree.

Linto returned to Montaup dispirited and broken. The only solace he had was that perhaps, like himself, Wampapaquan had eluded death in a miraculous fashion and was divinely chosen for a remarkable destiny yet to be revealed.

His reunion with Metacomet would be difficult. By now he would have heard the good news that Linto befuddled and embarrassed Patuckson and the English in the court of law. He would have heard the bad news that it did not matter, and all were condemned. Linto would deliver the horrible news that Tobias and Mattashunnamo had been executed, but, as expected, Tobias died with bravery and dignity. Linto would deliver the astoundingly good news that Wampapaquan's execution failed, and he was miraculously still alive. He would reveal the disastrous news that during Wampapaquan's hysterical rant, he told the English that Metacomet had ordered Sassamon assassinated. It had been an unimaginable two days, but somehow Wampapaquan's survival had given him hope. The miracle of the broken rope had given Linto hope.

Three sunrises later, a messenger from Plimoth arrived with four heavily-armed escorts. He found Metacomet and Linto and announced that the government of Plimoth Colony enthusiastically concurred with Linto. After solemn, earnest prayer and careful consideration, they accepted the indisputable message that hanging Wampapaquan by his neck did not meet with the Lord's approval.

Wampapaquan had been shot at dawn.

CHAPTER NINETEEN

PROVIDENCE

Brewster pensively contemplated his work. He took three steps back and hunched over to gain a different perspective. He lifted it high in the air and, closing one eye, peered at it accusingly, obsessively seeking any imperfection. He set it down and walked around it with a sense of pride and admiration.

It was an outstanding bucket.

It was another beautiful day in Providence and Israel Brewster felt satisfied. Sometimes he could scarcely believe that he, a defrocked minister with marginal eyesight who could barely drive a nail straight four years ago had achieved such a level of skill and craftsmanship. His spiritual life was an equally remarkable transformation.

Brewster was so impressed with Deputy Governor Easton, and so grateful for his friendship, that he attended another service with the Society of Friends. And then another. His sense of shock gradually transitioned to a sense of admiration. He was enthralled with the sincerity, the piety, and the candor. Did he attend worship daily, or even weekly? Probably not. Did he identify as a Quaker? No. Although continually impressed by the congregation, he never felt entirely at ease with the doctrine of pacifism. He would not abstain wholeheartedly from alcohol as their faith advocated. He yearned for a more formal, scripture-based mode of worship. And most of all, he missed his pulpit.

Since his encounter with John Easton, Israel Brewster had ceased numbing his brain with liquor. He still sparingly enjoyed the fine ales and wines of Providence, and he was known to occasionally hoist a mug of good cheer. But Israel Brewster would no longer see fit to squander his time.

Evenings were spent with a sense of devotion to the

community. He distributed food to the needy. He hauled firewood for widows. He taught the illiterate how to read. Some were English, but many were Indian. This newfound devotion felt right, and was deeply satisfying, but it would never compare to the sense of duty that brought him so much joy as an ordained minister. He had once been a shepherd with a flock.

In addition to simple, humble worship, and a sense of glorious peace, the Society of Friends in Providence offered Brewster another benefit, one he certainly did not anticipate. He was falling in love again.

During that first service, when Brewster felt as if his head would spin clean off his neck, he was too stunned and distracted to notice that the shockingly impertinent woman who dared to stand of her own free will, and dared to denounce the liquor, the arrogance, and the human bondage so pervasive in these New England colonies, was in fact, quite beautiful.

Constance Wilder was the twenty-four-year-old daughter of a curt, boorish and outspoken fisherman. Ezekiel Wilder, in fact, was a fisherman but now he owned and outfitted three separate boats. Despite his recent prosperity, he was *still* curt, boorish and outspoken, characteristics Brewster was surprised to discover in a middle-aged Quaker. Constance's mother had perished from influenza nine years ago.

Brewster reveled in the company of Constance and "Zeke." Never once was he made to feel like a disgraced, fallen outcast. He was never interrogated about Calvinist doctrine, or predestination, or original sin. Their conversations about politics, literature, and their Indian neighbors, however, often lasted far into the night. Zeke was very fond of Brewster, and most importantly, was thrilled to finally procure some reliable buckets and barrels for his fishing fleet.

Constance was quite tall and slender. Her red hair and hazel eyes complimented her fair skin beautifully. She had been courted by numerous gentlemen in Providence, all of whom eventually abandoned their efforts when they discovered they could not reconcile themselves to a romance with a woman who was outspoken, fiercely independent, and their intellectual superior. Brewster counted his blessings.

Israel Brewster had a new romance, a new profession, and a new sense of harmony. As he contemplated the beginning of another beautiful day, things became even better when he spied Easton entering the cooperage. Brewster was always awed by Easton's cordial, unassuming manner. Though he was the deputy governor, he never seemed hurried, distracted, or unwilling to lend his time. Brewster felt enormously indebted to him, and had no idea Easton was arriving to seek a favor.

"You there! Is that supposed to be a bucket, or is it an ugly helmet for your ugly horse?" Easton never tired of laughing about their first meeting, and tried to begin every conversation with *you there*. "If it's a helmet, I can take it off your hands for two pence. You can pay me now or next week."

"Oh, it's too fine a helmet for a mere horse. This is the special, ceremonial helmet designed for the deputy governor to wear in the performance of his regal duties." Brewster held it aloft. "All hail Governor Buckethead!" He was rewarded with Easton's legendary laughter.

"And how is your kindred spirit this week? You are aware that Deputy Governor Buckethead is authorized to perform weddings?"

"I was hoping my ugly horse could do the honors someday. But first he has to get elected."

Easton laughed so hard that Mr. Barlow had to peek around the corner to investigate the commotion. Easton then appeared serious. "Israel, I wish we could spend all day laughing and joking but another crisis is in our midst. I am fearful for all of New England." Brewster set the bucket down.

"Plimoth?"

"Have you heard?"

Brewster had remained intentionally and delightfully ignorant of Plimoth politics these last four years. He shook his head. "I haven't heard anything. More blasphemers and dissidents?"

"Did you ever work with John Sassamon?"

"Of course. He might be the most renowned Indian in the colony. His knowledge of scripture is most impressive."

"It is good to know he lived a Godly life because he is dead. They believe he was murdered." Stunned by the news, Brewster stepped away from his workbench and took a seat as Easton continued.

"He was found under the ice in a pond. Just south of Middleborough. Did you know Tobias? He was one of Metacomet's lieutenants." Brewster admitted he did not, and Easton continued. "Tobias and two others were charged with the murder. They were executed." Brewster hung his head and looked at his hands. He was saddened by the seemingly endless strife and turmoil.

"Israel, the story becomes even more extraordinary. There was a Wampanoag named Linto who spoke in court on behalf of the accused. Allegedly, he made Plimoth Court appear as an assembly of blundering buffoons."

Linto! Brewster snapped to attention upon hearing the name. "Linto! Linto served as counselor to the defense?" He was shocked by the news and yet he wondered why. He knew even four years ago Linto was unique. Brewster wished *he* could have found a way to reveal Plimoth Court as an assembly of blundering buffoons when he stood before them.

Easton continued. "The evidence was disgraceful. No

jury in the old world or new should have convicted those defendants. But convicted they were, and executed. And if the situation wasn't appalling enough, even the execution was botched."

"Botched? How do you botch an execution?"

"The rope broke. They were left with a poor, helpless young Indian, crying and wallowing on the platform. I believe he was actually Tobias' son. The poor soul was so delirious he cast aspersions of guilt upon his father and Metacomet."

"Metacomet?"

"The lad said Metacomet ordered Sassamon's assassination. I don't know if Plimoth found it credible or not, but they shot the poor lad all the same."

"Dear Lord." Brewster tried to grasp the enormity of this development. "The Wampanoag must be furious. Sassamon was an Indian. This should have been their crime to adjudicate." He pondered what could possibly happen next. "Is Plimoth going to try to convict Metacomet?"

"I can't imagine. Their actions are certainly difficult to predict, but even with their shockingly low threshold of evidence, I doubt the desperate ravings of a man with his head in a noose could suffice. Besides, how could they take him into custody?"

Brewster considered that last statement and tried to picture a hundred militiamen of the United Colonies marching into Montaup. "What are the Wampanoag going to do?"

"I think they are preparing for war. I pray I'm mistaken, but I don't believe I am. There has been far too much activity among all the Indian nations. Israel, I believe our duty is clear."

"Our duty? What duty do I have to Plimoth Colony?"

"Blessed are the peacemakers, for they shall inherit the earth. Have you ever heard that before, Reverend?" Even in jest, Easton knew the impact of his words.

"You want to try to reason with Plimoth? You certainly don't want me there."

"And they don't want a blasphemous Quaker heretic there either, even if he is a deputy governor. No Israel, we are going to Montaup. There must be a way to mediate this. I fear another Indian war could be the end of these colonies."

"You want me to go to Montaup?"

"You have served as a missionary to the Wampanoag, have you not? You may even know one or two?" Israel nodded his agreement and Easton appeared pleased.

"Excellent. We leave at dawn. I will tell Barlow you're on a mission for the deputy governor. And Brewster?" Brewster looked up expectedly.

"Don't forget your horse helmet."

CHAPTER TWENTY

MONTAUP

Linto bounced his son on his knee and tried to smile at Wawetseka. The events of the previous week had been devastating, and it was increasingly difficult to appear happy and carefree.

Although Metacomet was very magnanimous and commended Linto for his efforts in Plimoth, Linto could not forgive himself for his failure. He was haunted at night by visions of corpses swinging from nooses, and visions of Tobias' son shrieking in terror.

Linto no longer harbored any delusions about Metacomet's intentions. The earnest, somber Sachem he had served for so long was evolving into a violent, passionate warlord. He increasingly instilled a sense of fear and awe in Linto. Throughout the week neighboring tribes had sent warriors to confer and prepare with Metacomet, and he would lead them in the rituals of war. They would pray, coat their hands and faces in animal blood, and dance maniacally around a fire.

Metacomet grieved that Tobias was not by his side, and now there was another devastating absence. Mentayyup had fallen ill during this grave time, and had barely left his wetu for several days. Wawetseka had visited last night, and she had held his hand while listening to his breathing. She feared the worst.

Linto handed his son to Wawetseka and stepped outside. All around him firearms were being cleaned, hatchets were being sharpened, and longbows were being evaluated for range and accuracy.

Linto prayed incessantly. There was going to be a war, and there was no way the Wampanoag could win. No matter whether the Nipmuc stood at their side, or the Narragansett, or even both, Linto knew the truth. He had been in the inner sanctum of Plimoth. The English were plentiful, they were well-armed and well-fed, and Linto had no doubt the United Colonies of New England would stand as one against the savage menace. Even if nine out of every ten Englishmen perished, there were countless more waiting across the sea.

Linto stood there, alone, despondent, and unsure what to do. Then something wonderful happened. After the broken rope, he would forever be reluctant to think of things as "miracles," but this was indeed wonderful.

Throughout all of Montaup, the cry went out. "Englishman! Englishman! We have him! Englishman!" The lone Englishman was marched forward with his hands secured behind him. His captor could not have been more than sixteen summers, and his proud bearing and enormous grin gave the impression he had just captured the King of England.

The captor called out, and his voice reverberated throughout the village. "Linto! Linto!" Everyone within earshot swarmed to the Englishman, who had an ignominious hood draped over his head. His captor was ready to burst with excitement. "Linto! This English spy said you would speak for him! He was captured three miles from here! Where is Linto?"

Linto stepped forward and did not say a word. The young warrior forced his prisoner to his knees, and then removed his hood.

"Two Ponds!" Linto could not contain his ecstasy. He was older and chubbier, but there could be no mistake. Two Ponds was not dead of fever, and he was not in England. Disgraced or not, Two Ponds was right here. Linto knelt and embraced him.

Brewster saw his status instantly elevated from despised English spy to honored guest of the Sachem's counselor. He was offered water to drink and strawberries to eat, and he was led to Linto's wetu.

Brewster thought he would sob upon seeing Wawetseka again. The emotions of the healing ceremony ran deeply, and he recalled her prophetic words: "We shall meet again." Now there were two tiny youngsters to behold as well. Brewster had no doubt Linto and Wawetseka would create beautiful children one day, and they were here.

Wawetseka embraced Brewster tightly and held the embrace as she inhaled. She exhaled and released him, and evaluated what she had mysteriously ascertained. "You are at peace, Two Ponds. There was more pain since I left you, but you are now well." Brewster would never truly fathom the otherworldly insights of some of the native healers, but he was a testament to their abilities.

Brewster recounted the tale of his exile from Plimoth and how he had spent the last four years. He asked Linto to recount the events of his time in Plimoth. He then conveyed the purpose of his visit.

"Deputy Governor Easton of Rhode Island has led a delegation of five men here. You know he is a Quaker and sees the world differently than the United Colonies. He knows we are on the precipice of war, and he implores the Sachem for a last chance at mediation."

Linto nodded knowingly, and he brought Two Ponds to meet the Sachem.

Although on a mission of peace, Brewster felt an ominous sense of dread as he prepared to meet Metacomet for the first time. Linto made the introduction in the Wampanoag language and conveyed Brewster's intentions. Metacomet's powerful arms seized Brewster by the shoulders.

Metacomet stared intensely at Brewster, and did not say a word for at least three entire minutes, which felt like thirty to Brewster. The Sachem then closed his eyes, and with his hands still firmly clutching the Englishman's shoulders, he whispered, "tell me Wamsutta's dying words."

"You have offered me much but I have accepted nothing. You have seen this with your own eyes. Though my destiny is closed, my fault is with the heavens. I have not been corrupted or poisoned by the English. Ensure the people understand and bear no ill tidings."

Metacomet appeared deeply shaken and he nodded his head solemnly. He would trust Two Ponds, and he would listen to the Quaker men. Two Ponds would lead him to the meeting, but he would bring forty warriors, for his days of trusting the English government were over.

Three miles to the northwest, John Easton apprehensively scanned the horizon. He felt regret and guilt about sending Brewster alone to the Wampanoag, but Brewster insisted it was the best course, and he was very persuasive. Easton and his men had set a decent table, ensured there was bountiful food and drink, and all they could do was wait.

His heart leapt with relief as he surveyed the party of Wampanoag making their approach. After cordial greetings and introductions, the men were seated. Easton was delighted to meet the renowned Metacomet, and he was fascinated by Linto's masterful English. Easton soon realized Linto would be facilitating most of the discussions.

Easton quickly made his points. He stipulated that Plimoth had been very heavy-handed in their dealings with the Wampanoag. He believed they were grossly unfair in regard to the Sassamon affair. Easton knew the status quo concerning the sale of Wampanoag land was unfair and unsustainable. He suggested the conflict be mediated by neutral parties. Easton recommended the governor of New York, and perhaps a neighboring Sachem of Metacomet's choosing. Above all, he emphasized that war would be horrific, and it would almost certainly mean the destruction of the Wampanoag nation.

Metacomet listened intently and did not interrupt Easton. He occasionally nodded solemnly. After Easton finished, Metacomet spoke at length, and Linto translated. He was calm and thoughtful, but Easton was soon pessimistic about his prospects for peace.

"We are grateful that you, Governor Easton and our friend Brewster would make this journey. We know your thoughts and efforts are sincere, and we know you are desirous of peace. The Quaker people have always been most fair, even when the men of Plimoth had evil intentions toward us.

"Your suggestion for arbitration by other parties is most interesting, but we will politely decline. I know nothing of the Governor of New York, but we have learned that when land is concerned, the Englishmen tend to think with one mind. I know how we have been treated in the recent peace treaty, I know how we have been treated in the land deals, and I know how we have been treated in their courts of law.

"You may think us unwise and misguided to prepare for war, but I ask you, Easton my friend, to look at this world of New England from our view. When Bradford and old Winslow landed at Patuxet, did my father Massasoit, the greatest Sachem to walk these lands, make enemies of them? He could have scorned and reviled them. How easy it would have been to slay them all! But the great Sachem cared for the pitiful, starving English. He protected them and taught them how to feed themselves. Winslow the son is alive because of the Wampanoag.

"When my father perished and my brother Wamsutta ruled the Wampanoag, how did the English treat him? When he sold land to you, the Quaker men, he was marched off to Plimoth like a criminal, where he became sick, and later died. We place our faith and trust in Plimoth and pray he was not poisoned, but we will never accept the hideous manner of his death.

"And what of the land? The English take and steal and nothing is ever enough. Now the governor of Plimoth tells the

Sachem of the Wampanoag when and how he can sell the land? Prence the governor was fair and kind, but now he is with my father. Skunk Genitals Winslow is now governor, and he controls all our land as if it is his own.

"Even when the land is lawfully ours, it means nothing because the English cattle and pigs roam wherever they please. They destroy our corn and foul our water. Why are they not required to remain on their own land?

"And the English treat us like children. They poison our minds and our souls with intoxicating beverages so we lose our ability to reason, and then the English make devious trades when the Wampanoag are full of liquor. Then the English parade around and announce how pious and holy they are, and how we are drunken, Godless savages.

"Are you aware of how Godless savages are treated by English law, Governor? Nothing we say or do has any merit. Twenty of us can tell the truth, but if one praying Indian tells lies, that is good enough. What right did they even have to accuse Wampanoag men about Sassamon's death? It was an Indian affair. And what manner of men would hang three Wampanoag with no evidence whatsoever? I tell you, Governor, someone deserves to die for that broken rope travesty.

"You say we should crave peace because they are strong and we are weak? Because our people have been ravaged by the vile English diseases? Then perhaps they, the strong, should behave as Massasoit did and care for the weak. Perhaps they should conduct their affairs with peace and love like their big ancient book tells them to.

"I have spoken long enough, Easton. You are kind and wise to come here, but we begged the English for peace before, and we signed treaties, and then they treated us even worse. Easton, whether I am alive or dead next summer, the Wampanoag will not be English subjects, and neither will our allies.

"For if I continue to live under the English, I will have no nation left to rule. Just as the English fight for their king, I will die fighting for my father's kingdom."

CHAPTER TWENTY-ONE

MONTAUP

Metacomet had spoken his mind, and no one knew what to expect next. Deputy Governor Easton implored him to reconsider his position of rejecting independent mediation, but his efforts were, unsurprisingly, futile. Metacomet, with the aid of Linto's English translation, had spoken so articulately and so passionately that all the men from Rhode Island knew there was no hope.

Deputy Governor Easton thanked Metacomet for patiently listening to his words, and he thanked him for articulating his grievances so clearly. The two men embraced and Easton said he would be praying earnestly.

Brewster caught Linto's eye and approached. He wondered if they would ever see one another again.

"What do you think will happen, Two Ponds?"

"I think it is clear we're going to have a war. A bloody, devastating war." Brewster scanned the body of water below, and contemplated the journey by boat back to Providence. His first boat ride ever had been very enjoyable, much to his relief. Zeke would be delighted. "What will you do, Linto?"

"What will I do? What do you mean?"

"Will you carry a weapon and kill the English?"

"You are the second person to ask me that this week. I genuinely do not know. I suppose I will stay by the Sachem's side and do whatever he asks of me. What will you do?"

Brewster should have anticipated the question, but he could not conceal the fact that he hadn't even slightly considered it. Like Linto, he had no idea. He had made a home in a land of devout pacifism. Did he have any loyalty left to Plimoth? To the United Colonies? Did he feel any loyalty to England in this matter? Weren't the Wampanoag also English citizens?

Even if he chose to fight, what would he do? Would he serve as a chaplain? Could he resume his role as a militiaman? Perhaps his best contribution to the war effort would be sturdy, reliable barrels. He was still not prepared to accept the reality that the war was happening.

"Linto, there must be something that you can do or say. The Sachem still trusts you implicitly, does he not?"

Linto was tentative. "I think so. I have no reason to think otherwise."

"Then do something. Do anything. You have to find a way to stop this. If you tell him there must be peace because the Wampanoag will be slaughtered like the Pequot, wouldn't he believe you?"

"I think he would, but...I must choose my words carefully. I have...I have made a promise I cannot break, and that guides my path."

"I am begging you to find a way. This has to be stopped. We have to do better. Just look around this world."

"Look around?"

"Look at this *New* England my grandfather dedicated his life to. It was supposed to be above and beyond the old England. Winthrop talked about a city on a hill, a refuge for the Godly."

Brewster's voice was rising and he was consumed with passion. "It was to be a new society of worship, brotherhood, and piety. And what have these five decades brought us? War. Famine. Disease. Oppression. Hatred. No more, Linto. I cannot bear any more. I have lost my wife, my child, and my ministry and I cannot bear to see these colonies burn."

Once again, Linto felt the weight of the world upon his shoulders. There was no worthy reply he could give, so they embraced without a word. Metacomet and the warriors were heading back to the village, and Linto would have to catch up.

He said farewell to Two Ponds the best way he knew

how. *"But love ye your enemies, and do good, and lend, hoping for nothing again; and your reward shall be great, and ye shall be the children of the Highest. Amen."*

And Brewster watched Linto walk up the hillside.

Linto was speechless and pensive during the journey home. The warriors were beating their chests and singing chants of battle. There had to be a path to peace. Somehow these English would have to see that treating the Wampanoag with dignity was preferable to violent, bloody war. But he needed time and he had none.

He knew what he had to do that night. He had to be alone. Linto required complete solitude, and he told his Sachem and Wawetseka he would be going into the woods to fast and pray. He brought nothing except the means to build a small fire.

Linto was very tempted that evening to partake of some mystical herbs that could impart visions and prophecy. He decided against it as he built the fire. Linto sought clarity, and he prayed for a solution.

As he stared into the fire, questions consumed him like dried kindling. Was he really a powwas? If he was a mystical being, chosen for a divine purpose, why were Wawetseka's prophecies and powers so much stronger? Was it divine intervention that he saw Two Ponds at the missionary service and received the revelation about Wamsutta? Or was it merely coincidence? Perhaps the English found a way to murder Wamsutta that even Wamsutta was never aware of, and Linto's intervention was completely misguided.

How could Linto witness something as miraculous as the broken rope, only to see it mean nothing? What did their deaths really mean? Did Tobias actually kill Sassamon, or did his son merely think he could save his own life by telling Plimoth what they yearned to hear? Could Metacomet have possibly ordered it, or did Tobias merely make that up so his young accomplices would have no doubts as Tobias broke Sassamon's neck?

Linto agonized about what he believed. Did the English God love the Wampanoag as much as He loved the men and women of Plimoth? Why did so many die of plague? Perhaps these English with their magnificent ways really were God's chosen people. Linto felt like he had been seeking these answers for years, and he was no closer to the truth.

Linto meditated throughout the night. He desperately sought spiritual insight regarding his role in this world, in the Wampanoag nation, and in this war. He tried not to think of his children because he did not want to cry.

When Linto finally did think of his children, he was blessed with a divine epiphany. It was a solution to the problem, and it came from the Great Spirit. No, it did not come from the Great Spirit, because it was a falsehood. It was a flagrant, premeditated lie, and Linto was overjoyed. For he believed he had finally found a course of action that, while not eliminating the prospect of war, would almost certainly delay it. It would delay it possibly a week, maybe two. It would be long enough that he could talk with the Plimoth men. He had no idea what he would tell them. He would find something, anything in their Bible to convince them that war with the Wampanoag was sinful and unholy. But tonight, he had to sell his lie to Metacomet.

He extinguished the fire and smeared hot ash across his face. He tangled his hair and weaved it with mud. He did his best to look maniacal.

He staggered back to the village. It was probably three or four hours to sunrise and Metacomet was leading warriors from the Nipmuc and Narragansett nations in a war dance. They danced around a fire that was the height of a man, and the noise was deafening. Linto wasn't even certain he could get their attention.

He seized a torch and lit it. He held it high in the air and waved it. He took a deep breath. This would require an even bigger performance than his day at the Plimoth General

Court. He made sure he had Metacomet's attention.

"Hear me, one and all! Hear me, great and brave warriors, for it is I, Linto, the chosen son of the Abenaki, the lone survivor in the sea of death! I, Linto, upon whom the Great Spirit bestowed the revelation of Wamsutta! Linto, who has the power to master the English wicked tongue, and who exposes their falsehoods and deceptions in their own courts of law! Hear my voice!

"I have been fasting and meditating, and the Great Spirit has blessed me with a holy vision. We are ready for war with a vile and despicable enemy, but the Great Spirit demands we truly reveal their evil nature for all to see. Therefore, it has been blessedly revealed to me, that whomever fires the first shot of the war and slays the first man, is accursed, and their side will taste defeat! Victory shall be awarded to the nation that is restrained and disciplined, and does not fire the first shot in anger! It has been spoken, it has been revealed!"

Linto's trance was over, and he collapsed on the ground.

He was afraid to look up. He speculated on what would happen next. He assumed the young warriors would laugh unabashedly, and Metacomet would turn away in shame, disgusted at his antics. He wondered if he would be exiled like Two Ponds. Metacomet was urgently striding toward him.

Metacomet hunched over to speak. "Are you still with us Linto? Is the prophecy complete?"

Linto feared it might be sarcasm, but he had to sustain the deception. He blinked and tried to look disoriented. "Sachem, did I speak? Was the spirit truth revealed?"

A relieved smile lit up Metacomet's face. "Yes! The spirit world has not taken you! You revealed much to us. We have been blessed with divine guidance, and we owe it all to you. At our most critical hour, you have done the things we so needed. You have been chosen, Linto. We have always known it."

Linto gazed toward the sky, ostensibly to fortify the

ruse, but more importantly, he did not want the Sachem to see his face. For if there was ever a face filled with self-loathing, it was Linto's. What had he done? How could take what is holy and revered, and use it for disgraceful deception?

He quickly set aside his regrets. He had done it. He had done what needed to be done, and Two Ponds would be proud. There would be no killing this week, there would be no war. Wawetseka would be proud. Wawetseka. What would he tell her? She would want to know every detail, and she could see through falsehood like the sun seeing through the dark.

Metacomet was clearly no longer in the mood for the rituals and dances of war. He quietly withdrew to his wetu, and remained alone, deep in thought and meditation. Soon the sun rose, and the Sachem emerged. He knew he had to see his most revered, trusted warrior.

Mentayyup could scarcely sit up when the Sachem arrived. He looked worn and haggard, and Wawetseka had told both of them the end was near, and they should make preparations. Metacomet could not conceal his tears. He knelt one knee so he could address Mentayyup eye-to-eye.

"My greatest friend, our greatest soldier. The Wampanoag have one last duty to ask of you. You will have the most difficult task of all."

CHAPTER TWENTY-TWO

SWANSEA

John Salisbury was relieved. Yes, it was the Sabbath. He was well aware of that. But it was also a beautiful June afternoon, and there was only so much church a fourteen-year-old farm boy should have to endure during the summer.

His father, William, monitored his activity carefully during the service. During the fifty-minute dissertation on the book of Ezekiel, John feared he would incite his father's wrath with his incessant squirming. But much to his father's satisfaction, he had maintained the expected level of discipline and attentiveness, and the family was in good spirits.

There was a good deal of concern throughout the congregation about the Indian situation, but frankly, no more than usual. Tensions had been high for years, and the families of Swansea had learned to live with the situation, just as they had learned to live with blizzards, drought, and hailstorms.

The Salisbury family had arrived home after the sumptuous church luncheon. They intended to keep their chores and labor to an absolute minimum in accordance with the Sabbath. John had removed his church attire and had meandered to the acreage on the south side of the five-acre farm. He carried a musket and a hunting knife, and was planning to shoot a goose or two for dinner. His Sabbath routine, however, was instantly shattered.

John surveyed the pasture. Three cows were butchered and dead. Three hundred yards down the hill, he could see the tool shed of the Cobb family farm was on fire. Then he heard the horrible sounds.

At least three Wampanoag men were maniacally running across their farmland. They screamed their strange language and shrieked their ghastly war cry. In the distance, bells were ringing furiously, directing the townspeople to assemble behind the walls of the garrison. John watched in horror as the invaders set their barn alight and chased the horses away.

He stood completely motionless as he surveyed the scene. He could hear the cries of his father as he ran from the family home to retrieve him. *"John, this way! Hurry, John!"* But John Salisbury was frozen in his tracks. For a huge, imposing warrior was slowly marching toward him, and stopped a mere forty yards away from the youngster.

The hideous flames had now completely engulfed the Salisbury barn. The grim warrior eyed John, eyed the boy's musket, and resumed his march. The warrior was huge by Wampanoag standards, and older than most. John was shocked by how sickly he seemed, and he wondered if the invader even had the endurance to pursue him.

The invader did not relent. John raised his musket as his hands shook, and then he pointed it. After church John wanted to be ready for any manner of fowl, so the flintlock musket had been primed and ready. He rotated the cock to the full-cock position. The invader screamed a blood-curdling cry, raised his hatchet, and ran for John. John pulled the trigger.

The cock of the musket rotated downward, and the flint seamlessly struck the frizzen. Sparks flew everywhere, and the priming powder in the pan was instantly ignited. The flash made its way through the touch-hole, and the main powder charge was ignited. John had primed the musket perfectly. It made a deafening sound as it fired.

John missed horribly. The lead ball whizzed two feet above the invader's head.

He knew he could never reload a flintlock in time to make a difference even though he had the material. John clearly had three options. He could turn and run, he could attempt to bludgeon the invader with his musket, or he could unsheathe his hunting knife. He chose the first option.

His father closed fast and they soon stood together another forty yards from their approaching enemy. William Salisbury glared at the invader and was astounded. Rather than capitalize on the badly missed shot, he stood there dancing. He screamed at the heavens and danced in a circle with his hatchet held high. While William stood there with his mouth agape, John was crouched and re-loading. Powder and a new musket ball had been added. The flash pan was re-primed, and the frizzle was closed, and the musket was re-cocked. William stood in a defensive posture around his son, wielding a shovel in a threatening manner. And yet the invader danced. William wondered if he was intoxicated.

Finally, John stood. He was ready, and it appeared his adversary had wearied of the dance. The Salisbury men genuinely wondered if he would drop from exhaustion. He was now looking upward, and while interrupted by coughing fits, he was yelling words completely incomprehensible to them. Had they understood his language, however, they would have heard his final words.

"Wamsutta, my brother! Embrace my spirit! Massasoit, my Sachem, prepare my way!"

The invader whooped and raised his hatchet high in the air, and furiously ran at the Englishmen. John hesitated and his hands shook again. His father wanted to grab the musket but there would be no time.

"Shoot, John! Shoot now!" John closed one eye and fired.

Mentayyup stopped and grinned, for he knew his heart had been pierced. He previously had grave doubts if the English boy was up to the task, but Mentayyup now knew that even he, the greatest warrior of the Wampanoag, couldn't have loaded the musket that quickly and shot that accurately. He fell to his knees and looked to the heavens once more.

He had fulfilled his duty perfectly.

Throughout Swansea, homes were burning and livestock were butchered. News traveled like lightning throughout the colony, and the English prepared. This savagery would be avenged.

Back in Montaup, Metacomet tried to grasp what he had started. It had begun. Linto's prophecy had been carefully followed, and victory for the people would soon result. Tomorrow, Mentayyup's killers would be held to account.

The Sachem had allies throughout the land, and soon more would flock to his banner. There would be no more surrender to the English. He sat on the majestic quartz rock and thought about the future, and he sobbed. Metacomet thought about his father, his brother Wamsutta, Tobias, Mentayyup, and he wondered how many more would perish this summer. But he would never forget or forgive the English wickedness that caused all of it.

King Philip's war had finally begun.

Author's Notes

This is my first novel. I hope you have enjoyed reading it as much as I have enjoyed researching and writing it.

When I set out to write a historical novel, I wanted to choose a relatively obscure topic that the casual reader was not familiar with. When one considers the remarkable events and clash of cultures leading to King Philip's War, it is astounding it is not a topic of greater study and reflection.

Many of us are familiar with the satirical approach to colonial American history: The Pilgrims landed on Plymouth Rock in 1620. We signed the Declaration of Independence in 1776. During the intervening 150+ years…pretty much nothing happened.

This is a sad and unacceptable approach to our history. King Philip's War, relative to the native and colonial populations, was one of the most catastrophic wars in American history, and too many of us have never even heard of it.

After finishing a historical novel, the reader often wonders, "did these events really happen that way?" For the most part, in *My Father's Kingdom,* the answer is a resounding *yes.* The main characters of Israel Brewster, Linto, Jeremiah Barron, Mentayyup, and Wawetseka, as well as several minor characters, are fictional. In the pages of history, however, you will find the names of Massasoit, Wamsutta, Weetamoo, Metacomet, Wootonekanuske, John Sassamon, Tobias, Wampapaquan, Mattashunnamo, Patuckson, and Petonowit.

Students of history will also recognize the names of colonists Josiah Winslow (and his father), Increase Mather, Elder William Brewster, John Eliot, Thomas Prence, John Easton, and John Salisbury. Additionally, the geographic locations are historically based, except for Linto's fictional childhood village. Newport would probably have been a more accurate center of activity for John Easton, but I chose Providence for my book.

Some may point out some discrepancies in my descriptions of the Native Americans, and that is understandable. Technically, Massasoit and his sons were of the Pokanoket people, which were part of the Wampanoag nation. For the sake of simplicity, I've used the broader identity of Wampanoag. Additionally, the different families of languages (Algonquin, Massachusett) can cause confusion, so for the most part I described their language as "Wampanoag."

The death of Wamsutta, in my opinion, is one of the most intriguing events in American history. There are several contradictory accounts surrounding his last days. Some say he was marched off at gunpoint. Some say he died while imprisoned by the English. There are those who claimed he was with eight people at his hunting camp; others say eighty. Some accounts mention Winslow's home and others do not. He may have perished while enroute to Plimoth, whereas others attest he perished after falling ill and being permitted to go home. The question of whether he met with foul play has never been decisively answered, but the suspicions of his people were certainly a causal factor in the tensions leading to the conflict.

The death of John Sassamon and the subsequent executions in 1675 enraged Metacomet and were a major trigger for the war. Historical records convey that Tobias, Wampapaquan, and Mattashunnamo were tried for the crime and executed. There are varying historical accounts of the "bleeding corpse" evidence, as well as the contention that Patuckson owed a substantial gambling debt to the accused. There are also varying accounts of a broken noose and subsequent shooting.

Other historical events include the "black sheep" status

of the Plimoth Billingtons, the tale of the haughty Dorchester Puritans, the tragic life and execution of dissident Mary Dyer, Massasoit being nursed back to health by Winslow in 1623, and John Easton's attempts at preventing the conflict in 1675. Metacomet's list of grievances as conveyed to Easton are well documented in history. It should also be noted some scholars contend, that for some unknown reason, Metacomet genuinely believed whoever fired the first shot would lose the war.

The reader may also note the New England colonists in the seventeenth century definitely spoke and wrote quite differently than we do today (try reading Increase Mather's *A Brief History of the Warre with the Indians in New England)!* For literary purposes, I did not attempt to emulate this. I did, however, obviously adopt the old spelling of Plymouth.

I am not a historian and I've greatly enjoyed studying this period of history. *King Philip's War: The History and Legacy of the 17th Century Conflict Between Puritan New England and the Native Americans* by Jay Moore and the Charles River editors, is a terrific account of the conflict and the events leading up to it. The online *Plymouth Colony Archive Project* by Patricia Scott Deetz, Christopher Fennell and J. Eric Deetz is a phenomenal resource to understand how the men and women of Plimoth Colony lived and worked. The online nativeamericannetroots.com was instrumental in learning the Wampanoag perspective of these events.

I am looking forward to writing the next book in the series. **If you enjoyed this first installment and wish to provide feedback, please write a quick review at Amazon.com.**

Thank you
James W. George
January 2017

Made in the USA
Middletown, DE
16 April 2017